I0671356

Just Another

Damn

Love Story

A NOVEL BY

CALEB ALEXANDER

Copyright 2012

This book is a work of fiction. Any resemblance to real people, living or dead, actual events, establishments, organizations, and/or locales are intended to give the fiction a sense of reality and authenticity. Other names, characters, places, and incidents, are either products of the author's imagination, or are used fictitiously, as are those fictionalized events and incidents that involve real persons and did not occur or are set in the future.

Acknowledgments

First and foremost, I want to thank the Almighty Creator. It would take a lifetime to list all of the blessings that have been bestowed upon me. I know that during the darkest times in my life, it was He Who carried me.

To my loving wife, Jennifer; my wonderful daughter, Cheyenne; and my awesome sons, Curtis and Caleb.

To my mother, Gwen; my father, Charles; my sisters, Denise, Staci, Erin, Syidah; and my brother, Theron.

And a very special acknowledgment to my grandmother, Lillie.

I would also like to acknowledge Deborah and Deshawn for a smoking hot cover. And I would also like to give a shout out to all of the wonderful friends and family members who have blessed my life throughout the years. You know who you are. I owe so much to so many, that it would be impossible to to list all of you. So, I will simply say thank you.

Dedication

This book is dedicated to Black Love. There is no force on Earth more magical, more nourishing, more sustaining, more fulfilling, than Black Love. It was that love that sustained us through some of the darkest times in human history.

-And-

This book is also dedicated to the sisters who make that love so special, so enriching, so worthwhile, so magical. It is the love of a good Black woman that makes her man feel as though he can conquer the world. Thank you sisters, for being our sustainers, our healers, our partners, our inspiration, our motivation, our lovers.

Just Another Damn Love Story

CHAPTER ONE

Wolves. No, they acted more like Hyenas. Ravenous Hyenas, eyeballing a wounded gazelle, she thought. Their eyes rolled up and down her body with a lust-fulness that would have made a prostitute blush. She had become used to male executives checking out her goods, but nothing like this. Six men arrayed around a conference table, ogling her body, undressing her with their eyes, and licking their lips was too much even for her.

Kimberly Neel was a professional. A graduate of Princeton, she had been an advertising executive for the past four years, and was quite good at what she did. She had dealt with all the knuckleheads in that male dominated industry, including pulling a three year tour of duty on Madison Avenue for one of the largest advertising firms in the country. She left Madison Avenue when the opportunity arose to join Mocha. Mocha was the largest African

American woman's magazine in the world. Six million subscribers, and a world wide circulation of over ten million. In the world of fashion, cosmetics, and entertainment, Mocha was a veritable powerhouse. And now, here she stood, trying to get a bunch of men to buy ad space. Men who hadn't heard a single word she said since her presentation started.

"And so you see, gentlemen," Kimberly continued. "Mocha has had similar success in the past. We have increased the exposure of companies similar to yours by two hundred percent, which in turn, resulted in a revenue increase of roughly thirty percent for those businesses. Advertising in Mocha, has been a winning proposition for all of our clients."

Ken, the vice president of marketing for the company, lifted his ball point pen into the air and posed a question. "I'm really not sure how this will benefit us."

If you had been listening, instead of staring at my breast you would have understood, Kimberly thought. She smiled politely at the V.P., and then drew in a deep breath.

"Your company has a children's clothing line also." Kimberly explained. "Well, who do you think makes those purchases? It's the women, the mothers, the aunts, the god mothers, the sisters, who all read our magazine. Same thing goes for your male clothing line. A lot of times, it's the wives, the girlfriends, or the mothers shopping for their high school age children who are purchasing your products. Our magazine can help you reach those potential buyers."

"I'm impressed," said Mark, closing his marketing folder. He was the president of the company, and his word carried the most weight. "My only problem, is that Mocha is so expensive. Twenty five thousand dollars is more than we traditionally spend for a one page add in a single issue. We get better rates from Source, Vibe, even XXL. All of them charge less, and they market directly to our consumers. We are an urban clothing line after all."

He had her reeling. He was right. Mocha was more expensive than all of the others. And, those others did showcase his wares directly to his target market. She had to think fast.

"Mark, what you say is absolutely true, Mocha *is* more expensive than the others. But that's because you pay for what you get. Mocha is read by consumers who actually go out and buy things. It's not read by teeny boppers more interested in rap articles and bling-bling dreams. Mocha is going to market your clothing to a different, more upscale clientele. It's going to expand your market. You already have the teeny bopper market. They're going to wear your clothing, because this or that rapper wears it. But to move into the minds of the suburban mothers who buy clothing, is something completely different. Let's keep it real here. Kids can't afford your sixty or seventy dollars jeans, but their parents can. Let's put your brand in the minds of those parents."

Mark nodded and rose from the conference table. "Kim, we thank you for coming. Naturally, we'll have to discuss this before we make any type of commitment. But you can rest assured, you have my vote."

Kimberly extended her hand, and Mark shook it.

"Thank you so much for your time," Kimberly told him. "Thank you all. I believe that you'll be very happy with the results that your ad dollars will generate at Mocha, and I very much look forward to working with you in the future."

"I look forward to working with you," Ken told her, lifting an eyebrow suggestively.

He made her head spin. Every time she looked at him, he reminded her of Brother man from Martin. Sure, he was Brother man in a Sean Jean suit, but he was a nuisance nonetheless.

Kimberly collected her belongings, and placed them in her Mont Blanc briefcase, as the company executives filtered out of the room. One of them lingered behind.

"Hey," Nelson called out to her. "Nelson Robins, Vice President in charge of purchasing and acquisitions."

Kimberly shook his hand. "Pleased to meet you."

"I was thinking," Nelson continued. "How about discussing your proposal over a nice quiet dinner?"

"I've already discussed the proposal," Kim told him. "You were listening, right?"

Nelson shrugged. "We can go to dinner, and discuss my support for your ad proposal."

"And if we don't go to dinner, I'm sure that I'll have your support anyway, right?" Kimberly asked, lifting an inquisitive eyebrow.

Nelson shrugged. "I wouldn't bet the house on it."

"That's what I thought." Kimberly lifted her

briefcase and turned toward the door. "Nelson, as far as your chances go, for taking me out to dinner…"

"Yeah?"

"I wouldn't bet the house on it." She turned, and exited the room.

*****

Old Palm Gold Club was one of the most expensive, most luxurious, and most exclusive golf clubs in the country. The club was home to an exclusive Raymond Floyd Signature Design 18-hole championship golf course, while the clubhouse itself was reminiscent of Palm Beach's "Golden Age." The old world Mediterranean architecture bespoke of an elegance and distinction that was timeless. Luscious travertine and marble floors, hand-fired clay tile roof, massive stone arches and fireplaces, and hand-forged wrought iron chandeliers could be found throughout the establishment.

It was on the ninth hole where Sterling Williams, owner of men's fashion powerhouse, Vespasian, was golfing and meeting with his best friend and legal counsel, Wilson Wealth.

"I still say, we should launch our women's casual and formal wear lines within the next twelve months," Wilson suggested.

Sterling swung his three iron at tiny Titlist ball, missing it by a couple of inches. "Shit!"

Wilson laughed.

"You did that on purpose," Sterling said with a smile.

"I didn't tell you to swing," Wilson protested. "Anyway, would you just put the club down and listen to me."

"What's the rush?" Sterling asked.

"Have you seen the numbers?" Wilson asked. "The numbers for women's fashion are way up, and continuing to rise. While our existing sales, are climbing only slightly. Right now, we are in the beginning stages of growing stagnant. We are going to be known as maker of expensive suits, for stuffy old businessmen. While Sean Jean, Calvin Klein, D&G, Armani, Ralph Lauren, Prada, Versace, Brioni, and Kiton, are going to control the young, hip part of the men's fashion industry."

"And what does this have to do with launching a women's clothing line?" Sterling asked with a smile.

"Right now, we only make women's dress shoes, handbags, purses, and business suits," Wilson explained. "We need to become a full fledged fashion house, attracting both sexes, and generating some heat across our entire lineup. For Pete's sake, Sterling, on our men's side, we only make business suits, polo shirts, and black tie attire. We don't even have our own line of dress shirts, socks, or ties! We need to expand our men's side, and launch a full fledged women's line."

"And you want to get this up and running within a year?" Sterling asked. "We don't have any designers on board, we don't even have anyone in mind to help put this thing together and run it. Do you know how long it will take just to get a staff together, to run a women's fashion house? That alone will take six months to a year. And then to get the designs picked, finalized, and to the manufacturers?"

"Sterling it's simple," Wilson said, exhaling. "We either expand, or the company dies. We need the young hip market, and we need to capture the women's market. It has to be the next big thing to rock a Vespasian purse, or some Vespasian knee high leather boots. Imagine Mary J. Blige walking on stage to pick up an award, while rocking a pair of thigh high Vespasian leather boots and a Vespasian form fitting sweater dress, or a matching Vespasian leather dress. Imagine millions of young teen age girls running to Saks, or Neiman Marcus, or Macy's to pick up the latest Vespasian purse with colorful ducks or crayons, or colorful V's on it."

"When I invited you down to Palm Beach, it was to golf, and go fishing with me on my yacht," Sterling said with a smile. "Not to spend the entire weekend talking business."

"Can't help it." Wilson shrugged.

Sterling shoved his golf club into his custom crocodile skin golf bag. "When I get back to the house, I'm going to relax by my swimming pool, have the masseuse give me a relaxing massage, and fall asleep until my plane leaves for New York. During that time, I don't want to hear another word about business."

"In that case, I better get it all in right now," Wilson told him. "I had Natalie pick up the new Vespasian leather handbag from the manufacturer's office before I left."

Wilson went into his golf bag, and pulled out a brown leather handbag with gold V's printed on it. He handed it to Sterling, and then pulled out a second handbag. This one was white, with green, red, yellow, orange, and blue V's printed all over it."

Sterling examined both bags and nodded. "I like. The only problem is, the mutli-color bags are out of season."

"Yeah, but not these," Wilson said with a smile. He flipped the multi-color handbag inside out, revealing the fact that it was reversible. The outside of the bag was now lavender, with glow-in-the-dark multi-color V's printed all over it. "We are going to own the teen age and young adult market with this bag."

Sterling threw his head back in laughter. "I knew there was a reason why I pay you so much money."

"Sterling, this is just the beginning." Wilson told him. "Go along with me on expanding our men's line, and on developing a full fledged women's line, and we are going to dominate the market."

"When we get back to New York, I'm going to find a new general counsel for the company," Sterling told him.

Wilson frowned. "Why? What'd I do wrong?"

"You're being fired from being the company attorney, because I'm making you a vice president."

Wilson wrapped his arms around his friend. "I don't know what to say."

"Say nothing," Sterling said, embracing his friend. "I should have done it a long time ago."

"Thank you."

"Don't thank me just yet. This new expansion project, it's your baby. You make it happen. But, if it crumbles, then you're back to being the company attorney."

"Thanks, Sterling. I won't let you down."

Sterling nodded. "Now, just do me a favor."

"What's that?"

"Let me enjoy the little bit of time that I have left down here in Florida. No more business for now."

Wilson smiled and nodded. "No more business."

Just Another Damn Love Story

Chapter Two

The new headquarters for Mocha Magazine were the twenty fifth floor of the Time Life Building. The spanking new headquarters came courtesy of the magazine's new owners, AOL Time Warner. AOL Time Warner had plenty of money, and could afford to house their acquisitions in nothing but the best. It was a far cry from the magazine's early days, when it was struggling to stay afloat. They were lean days, but they were the days that Laquisha remembered fondly.

Laquisha Denny started Mocha while she was still in college. She worked full time while going to school, and poured all of her resources into her tiny magazine. She shopped it at beauty shops throughout Harlem, and then Brooklyn, and finally Queens, before taking it to Jersey and then Philly. By the time Mocha hit B-More, and D.C. she actually was averaging about seventy pages a month in the magazine, and thought that she was hot stuff.

Mocha went national after hooking up with a couple of college buddies who were now working for various distributors to large national chain stores. They helped get Mocha on the shelves in Houston, Dallas, Chicago, Atlanta, and Los Angeles. The rest was history. Mocha spread across the country faster than a Brad and Angelina rumor. And then the big dogs came sniffing at her door.

She turned them down at first. Peterson's, Murdoch's outfit, Buffet's group, various media investors from England, France, and India. Finally, AOL Time Warner came with a check that was just too damn large to say no to. Plus, they allowed her to stay on as editor-in-chief, with full creative and executive control over the magazine. She could hire and fire, allocate their dollars any way she saw fit, and she had final say over what went into the magazine that she poured her heart and soul into building. It was a win-win situation. But still, she was a little bitter.

The check had been nice, but still, it was peanuts compared to the numbers that the magazine was doing now. She kicked herself in the shin everyday for selling out. The millions that the magazine was raking in monthly could have been hers, all hers. But she took the quick payout, and now she had to come to work everyday and watch someone else reap the benefits of her hard work. Perhaps that was why she was pissed off all of the time, she thought. She knew that she was bitter, and she knew that she came across as a bitch to her employees. But after all, watching someone in Atlanta make millions of dollars each month, off of a company that she built, would piss off even the most saintly person. And Mother Teresa she was not.

Laquisha had grown up in Pink House. At least until her parents divorced, and then she moved in with her grandmother in Do-or-die-Bedstye. She had it rough. Crooklyn was no joke back in the day. Money was tight, school was a survival camp, and dodging the bullets and the dope boys on the way home everyday was like an Olympic sport. It was enough for her to not get pregnant like her older sister, and an even bigger accomplishment to graduate from high school. Managing to go to Community College of New York, and then NYU was something bordering on miraculous in her neighborhood. But she made it. And now, she was peering out of the corner office, on the twenty fifth floor, of the Time Life Building.

"Come in!" Laquisha barked, as the knock came to her door.

Kimberly timidly pushed open the door, and she and her co-workers crept into their boss's office.

"Come in and close the door, ladies, and Jerome," Laquisha told them. She waved to some chairs arrayed around her office. "Have a seat."

"Ladies would have been acceptable," Jerome told her.

"Jerome, *you* are gender confused," Laquisha told him. "I am not."

"Who said I was confused?" Jerome shot back. "Having this big old penis does not make me a man. I'm every women…"

Laquisha held up her hand silencing him. "We are not going to have this conversation today! I called y'all asses in here to talk about some numbers. Numbers that are way down. When the numbers are down, revenue is down, and that means, my income that's based on a percentage of what this magazine pulls in, is down. Y'all playing with my money, and we all know, that Laquisha don't play with her money!"

"I just pulled in the Sean Jean account!" Pamela protested.

"That was last month," Laquisha told her.

"But they took out a year's worth of adds!" Pamela shot back. "That was a three hundred thousand dollar score!"

"So what!" Laquisha told her. "Do you think that you're supposed to just sit on your ass for the rest of the year?"

"I pulled in the MAC account before that," Pamela told her. "And I scored Revlon before that!"

"What have you done for me lately?" Laquisha asked. "See, you made me get all Janet on you! You know I hate to bring out my Janet."

"I scored the Tommy Hilfiger account just last week," Jerome told her.

"Yeah, and we had to discount five thousand dollars a month to get it!" Laquisha shouted. "Don't you even mention that bootleg deal you made with RJ Reynolds! Some of our other advertisers were pissed about that cigarette ad. Not to mention corporate, *and* some of our readers."

"I got Revlon," Jerome added.

"Two months ago!" Laquisha told him. "Don't make me go Janet on you!"

Kimberly raised her hand.

"What?" Laquisha shouted.

"I got a lead from Mercedes, and from Allstate,"Kimberly told her.

"What happened to the Black Expressions deal?" Laquisha asked, tilting her head to the side and pursing her lips.

"The meeting went well," Kimberly said nervously. "I'm still waiting to hear back from them."

"What else you got coming up?" Laquisha asked.

"I have meetings with Lays, with the Air Force, with Pepsi, and with Soft Sheen Carson," Kimberly told her.

"And you?" Laquisha asked, turning toward Jerome.

"I'm meeting with the Army today," Jerome told her. "If they don't ask, I won't tell."

Pamela and Kimberly burst into laughter.

"Don't encourage him!" Laquisha shouted. "What else you got? People, you are my advertising executives. You are the *life blood* of the magazine. If you don't produce, we don't survive!"

"I'm meeting with American Airlines tomorrow, Lustrasilk on Tuesday, McDonald's on Tuesday afternoon, Pantene on Wednesday, and Victoria Secret on Thursday."

Laquisha nodded, and turned toward Pamela.

Pamela exhaled. "I got Walmart on Tuesday,

Jeep on Wednesday, S C Johnson & Sons on Thursday, GMAC on Friday morning, Pfizer on Friday afternoon, and Clinique this afternoon."

Laquisha clapped her hands together. "Let's get out there and get that money."

Pamela, Kimberly, and Jerome turned and headed for the door.

Jerome shoved Kimberly and Pamela. "You heard her. You bitches better get out there and get pimp Quisha's money!"

The three of them broke into laughter as they exited the office and headed down the hall.

*****

Sterling packed away more of his belongings into the cardboard box on his desk, so that he could clear out his office for Wilson. He had decided to move Wilson into *his* office, and finally clean out the large corner office that the company had been using for storage. He would take *that* office, and move the boxes that now occupied it, into a proper storage closet elsewhere in the building.

Wilson strolled into the office carrying a white

25

handbag and matching white leather trench. Both had large gold letters printed all over them.

"What is SPQR?" Sterling asked.

"It's the coat of arms of the Roman Empire," Wilson explained.

"White with gold letters, I love the look, love the design of the bag and the trench, but what's with those letters in particular?" Sterling asked, lifting an eyebrow.

"Sterling, we pretend that our main corporate headquarters is in Milan, just so people will believe that Vespasian is an *Italian* company," Wilson explained. "We have to put out merchandise that pays homage to Italian history or that has Italian themes."

"Yeah, but why so over the top?"

Wilson laughed. "You're used to bespoke men's suits. All dark and double breasted. Your idea of fashion excitement is adding subtle pinstripes. Let me handle the women's fashions."

Sterling waved his hand. "You got it."

Marleena, Sterling's secretary, strolled into the office holding up a pair of white, open toed, high heels with a gold SPQR logo as the toe strap.

"Now those are fly!" Sterling told them. "Is this the stuff we talked about doing months ago?"

Wilson nodded.

"It turned out great," Sterling said while nodding. "Any luck finding a designer?"

"Not yet," Wilson exhaled, and plopped down in the chair behind the desk. "I'm still searching for one with that right look. I interviewed three designers this morning."

"How's the executive search coming along?"

Wilson shook his head.

"Stay at it, we'll find someone."

"You ready for the rest of the material?" Wilson asked.

Sterling turned, leaned back against the desk and folded his arms. One by one, various models strolled into the room, showcasing Vespasian's latest designs.

"Love that suit," Sterling told Marleena. "Take notes. We need a three button, English version, in the same material. This pants suit coming up, needs to be flared more at the ankle. Also, I want the same jacket, but with a straight pants leg variation, and also a variation with a long skirt. Love that suit. That one is perfect as well."

"Marleena, are these Ford models, or the new ones from Wilhelmina?" Wilson asked.

"Wilhelmina," Marleena told him. "Also, Fed

Ex delivered the ties from the manufacturer today."

"I want to see them after this viewing," Sterling told her.

"They probably delivered the scarves as well," Wilson added.

"We are really going through with this expanded women's line?" Sterling asked.

Wilson nodded. "It's about time."

"I showed the reversible purse to my daughter, the one with the glow-in-the-dark V's, and she went crazy over it," Marleena told him. "I think you have a hit on your hands with that one."

"What's this?" Sterling asked, stopping one of the models. He clasped her forearm and held up her hand.

"That's our wrist bag," Wilson explained. "It's a tiny handbag, attached to a thick bracelet. It'll be great for formals, or for anywhere women just want to carry a small fold.

Sterling nodded. "I like it."

Marleena nodded. "Another hit."

"And now, for the *coup de grace...*" Wilson stood, and waved his hand towards the door. "Our company's first take on the little black dress!"

A model strutted into the office wearing a form fitting black dress that stopped at her knees.

Sterling nodded.

"With the right accessories, you can wear it to work, change accessories and wear it to a cocktail party, change accessories and wear it to a formal or to church," Wilson said excitedly. "It's stylish, versatile, and absolutely stunning!"

"Who did it for us?" Sterling asked.

"That little Italian girl that works in our Milan office," Wilson explained.

"She's good," Sterling told him. "Well, I like what I've seen so far. Especially the men's line up, and the new handbags and shoes."

"Well, you know where to sign," Wilson told him. "We can get everything into production within two weeks."

Sterling nodded. "You sign. That'll be your new job. And we need to get on the ball, and get some designers in here and get this thing off the ground. Also, we need to find someone to run the whole kit and caboodle. Think we can steal someone from another fashion house?"

"With what you pay?" Wilson asked with a smile. "Not likely."

Sterling laughed. "Let's just keep our eyes and our options open."

Just Another Damn Love Story

Chapter Three

Kim absolutely loved her apartment. She had managed to secure a primo two bedroom apartment smack dab in the middle of Times Square. Her building, 1600 Broadway, was legendary for its location and views. Her apartment over looked the famous Candy Factory just off of the square. In fact, she could take in the New Years celebration from the comfort of her living room, or venture out onto her balcony to listen to the countdown and watch the ball drop.

1600 Broadway had concierge service, on-site parking, a rooftop swimming pool and recreation area, and an in building spa and workout center. Her father's credit and financial support had really helped her living situation. She wouldn't trade her apartment for any in the world.

Kimberly's furnishings were straight out of Ikea. They were very sheik, very modern, very chic.

She had a cream colored curving sectional that took up most of her living area. She had bamboo end tables and a bamboo coffee table that matched the bamboo flooring of the apartment, as well as the bamboo cabinetry in her kitchen. Her kitchen was a study in modernity itself. In addition to the Bamboo cabinetry, it boasted concrete counter tops, and stainless steel Viking appliances. Her dining area was taken up by a space saving glass dining table with ultra modern birch wood chairs. Above the concrete mantle of her fireplace, rested her pride and joy; a seventy-two inch flat panel television. The T.V. had been a house warming gift from her mother. Otherwise, it would have remained in the electronics store. There was no way she would have been able to spend six grand on a television.

Kimberly's bedroom was decked out like that of an Egyptian princess. She loved black and gold, and she loved ancient Egyptian artifacts and artwork. Her bed was a platform bed that rose only inches off of the floor. On top of that flat platform, she had her memory foam mattress, clad in gold and black silk sheets, and covered with a thick gold and black comforter with hieroglyphics and pyramid motifs on it. The bed dressing matched her curtains, as well as her black and gold artwork. On the wall, was her other pride and joy; a sixty-five inch flat panel television.

Kimberly strolled across the floor of her apartment, into her kitchen, and fixed herself a nice hot cup of espresso. The Miele espresso machine had been a gift from her aunt, and it turned out to be one of the best house warming gifts in the history of Western Civilization. The stainless steel machine made the best espressos, lattes, and coffees in the world. It really came in handy on cold winter mornings and back breaking days like today; days when she needed to simply lay back in her leather recliner and relax.

Her trip to her recliner was interrupted by the telephone.

"Hello?" Kim said, lifting her cordless to her ear.

"Kimberly, darling, how are you?"

Kimberly rolled her eyes and exhaled forcibly. "Mother, how are you?"

"Just sitting in my sun room, worried sick about you," Mrs. Neel told her.

"Why are you worried about me?" Kim asked. "I'm fine."

"How would we know?" Mrs. Neel snapped. "You never call, you never come by. No e-mails, not even a lousy postcard."

"A postcard? Mom, I live in Manhattan, you live in Westchester, why would I send you a postcard?"

"You could send a telegram or a letter by pony express for all I care. Your father and I just want to hear from you."

"Mother, I just saw you in church last week."

"But you missed service yesterday," Mrs. Neel countered. "We hadn't heard from you, anything could have happened. We worry about you so much. I mean, living in the city is so dangerous, especially for a *single* woman."

Kimberly exhaled and got comfortable. She knew what was coming next. Her mother's diatribe about marriage was an almost weekly ritual.

"I'm fine, Mother."

"No, you're not fine, Kimberly!" Mrs. Neel said forcefully. "You're living in the middle of all those wild and raunchy people, you've tossed away your only immediate prospect for a husband, you're stuck in a dead end job, and you refuse to go back to school and get your MBA or your CPA. I don't know what to do."

"There is nothing for you to do, Mother. Times Square is not filled with raunchy and dangerous people, it's just full like that on New Years. I did not throw away my only prospects for a husband. John and I split, because he had way too many issues, way too many children, and way too many baby mommas. And my job is not a dead end job, I'm an ad executive at one of the largest magazines in the country."

"John is an orthopedic surgeon, for Pete's sake!"

"Yeah, with three different baby mommas! One of whom slashed my tires, and another who threw a brick through my car window and keyed my car door!"

"And you blame him for their behavior?"

"I just couldn't deal with the drama anymore, Mom. The stalking, the telephone calls, the messages left at my job. It was too much. And he wasn't helping to control the situation."

"You let a good man get away, because you weren't willing to fight for him?"

"Mother, please. Not this conversation again. I've had a rough day."

"Well, if you were the wife of a doctor, you wouldn't have to work at that dead end job."

"Mother, I love my job. It's challenging, and rewarding, and…"

"And it leaves you exhausted and broke."

"I'm not broke."

"Do you need money?"

"I could use some," Kimberly said softly.

"Ah-ha!" Mrs. Neel told her. "See, if you go back to school, get your MBA or your CPA, then you could get a job that pays some *real* money. And, if you furthered your education, it would dramatically improve your chances of getting into the Links."

"Mother, who said that I wanted to join the Links?"

"Don't be silly, dear. Everyone wants to join the Links."

"You may find this hard to believe, but not everyone wants to join your group of gossiping old women."

"Kimberly!"

"Mother!" Kimberly exhaled. "Look, Mom, I have to go. I have something cooking on the stove. Tell Dad I love him, and I'll talk to both of you later. Love you."

Kimberly hung up the telephone before her mother could get another word in. She reclined in her chair, lifted her warm espresso, and turned her attention toward her television. A nice Lifetime movie would do her some justice right now. She needed to see something about women overcoming, overpowering, or snipping off the protruding parts of a lousy, cheating man. Hopefully, that man would be a cheating orthopedic surgeon with way too many ex-wives.

*****

Sterling strolled through the park toward the playground. It was a playground he knew well, as it served as his weekly pick-up spot for his most cherished possession in the world; Sterling Williams III.

"Daddy!" Sterling III raced to his father and leaped into his arms.

Sterling lifted his son into the air and spun him around. "Third!"

Sterling planted kisses all over his son's face. He was too much in rapture to notice the approach of the boy's mother.

"You're late," Carmela said sternly.

"I am not," Sterling protested.

Carmela peered down at her wrist watch.

"You were supposed to be here at two o'clock."

"For Pete's sake, Carmela, its two minutes after two right now!" Sterling told her.

"Which means you're late!" Carmela told him.

"I'm not going to let you ruin my day," Sterling told her. "Me and Third are going to spend some time together in the park."

"Look, I don't even have to let you do this!" Carmela reminded him. "It's not the weekend. I'm just being nice and letting you spend time with him, since we were going to be here today anyway."

Sterling held out his palms, calming the situation. "Okay, I know. I thank you for it. We're just going to head over to the swing and spend some time together."

Carmela peered down at her watch. "You got fifty five minutes left." She turned, seated herself on a nearby park bench, and engrossed herself in the novel she brought along.

Sterling wrapped his arm around Third, and the two of them headed off to a nearby play area.

"So, how have things been going?" Sterling asked.

Third shrugged his shoulders. "The same. Mom made me go to church Sunday."

"That's good. You're supposed to go to

church."

"But when I got home, my X-Box messed up."

"What happened to it?"

Third shrugged his shoulders again. "I don't know, it just stopped working."

"Well, it just so happens, that I went online today, and I checked a certain young man's grades, and they were all A's."

Third smiled and nodded.

"So," Sterling continued. "I think a brand new X-Box can be arranged. If I would have known you needed one, I would have brought it today. But, since I didn't know, I only brought this." Sterling reached into his pocket and pulled out a video game.

Third instantly snatched it out of his hand. "Madden '13! All right!" He again wrapped his arms around his dad.

"I wish you would call me when you need something," Sterling told him.

Third nodded. "I didn't need anything."

"You needed a new X-Box."

"Mom said that a new X-Box is a want, not a need," Third explained. "She said that it was a privilege."

Sterling laughed and nodded. "Your mom's right. You make sure that you always listen to her.

You be a good son, and you do what your mother tells you to do."

"I want to live with you, Dad."

"You can stay with me on the weekends like you've been doing."

"But I want to stay on the weekdays too."

"Your mom wouldn't go for that," Sterling told him. "I would love to have you live with me all of the time, but I can't. Your mom loves you just as much as I do, so we have to share you."

Third nodded. "But if we all lived together again, then both of you could share me all of the time."

"Yeah, and that's a really good idea," Sterling said uncomfortably. "But, your mother and I have to have different houses right now."

"Why?"

"Because, we like to do things different. Your mom has certain ways of running a house, and your dad has his ideas about how things should go. So, instead of arguing about which way to do things, we each have our own house so that we can do things the ways we like."

"My teacher says that everyone should compromise."

Sterling threw his head back in laughter. "You

kids are getting sharper with each passing generation. Here, climb onto this swing so I can push you."

Third seated himself on the swing, and Sterling pushed from behind.

"I'm really proud of you, Third. You're doing really well in school, and you're doing really well at home. You help your mother a lot, and you're a fantastic kid. You're the best son in the whole world."

"Are you buttering me up?" Third asked.

Sterling laughed and rubbed his son's head. "No, I'm not buttering you up! I'm just telling you how fantastic you are. You make me the happiest dad in the world, and I'm just letting you know it, that's all."

"Can we go get ice cream?"

Sterling peered at his watch. "We'll ask you mother if she'll let us go for some ice cream."

"You think she will?"

"Maybe, if we let her go with us."

"I love you, Dad."

"I love you too, Third."

Chapter Four

Chin Chin's was Manhattan's premier spot for upscale Asian cuisine. Nestled between 2nd and 3rd Avenues, the restaurant was patronized by the Big Apple's elite. Wall Street movers and shakers, as well as sports stars, music artist, and runway superstars could be found sitting in the restaurant's VIP section throughout the day. The restaurant's delectable cuisine, as well as the potential for star gazing, was what made it one of the city's trendiest spots. It was also what made the restaurant a favorite meeting place for Kimberly and her girlfriends.

"Hey!" Kimberly rose from the table and greeted Mia, who was the first to arrive.

"Hey, girl!" Mia said, hugging Kim. "I thought that I was early."

Mia was half Malaysian, and half Philippine. Her skin was a deep caramel, while her hair was long and wavy. She had full lips, hazel eyes, and thick natural eyebrows. She could have continued to model, and been a runway superstar, but instead her dreams took her to Princeton, where she majored in political science. She graduated from college at the age of eighteen, and received her Masters at the age of twenty. By the time she turned twenty one, she had her Ph.D in Political Science, and was a rising star in New York's State Democratic Committee. Her current job was with the National Democratic Party's New York office.

"Let me look at you!" Kimberly told Mia, lifting her arms up. "Girl, love that Obama '12 t-shirt! That is so cute!"

"Twenty-twelve, girlfriend!" Mia said, hi-fiving Kim.

"Are we gonna get it done?" Kimberly asked.

"We gone get it done!" Mia told her.

Mia had been one of Kim's best friends since Princeton. Mia had been in graduate school, while Kim was an undergrad. But they were the same age, and they were dating roommates across the campus. Mia's dating of Black men, often earned her the consternation of sisters on the street, and often brought Kim into the mix in defense of her friend.

"Hey, girlfriends!" Brittany squealed as she

walked to the table and hugged Kim and Mia.

"Hey, girl!" Kim said, exchanging hugs.

"Hey, girlfriend," Mia said, hugging Brittany in turn.

The three of them took their seats, just as the waiter approached and left menus around the table.

"You cut your hair!" Kimberly declared.

Brittany patted her pixie cut and modeled her new hair style for them, while they pretended to ooooh and aaaaah. Brittany was the silly one of trio. She had a goofy sense of humor, and took things much less seriously than the other two. She was white, privileged, and rich. Having light, naturally blond hair, crystal blue eyes, a gorgeous shape, and a degree from Princeton gave her an advantage in life that most would die for. The fact that her parents owned Sherwood Hotels didn't hurt either. She could afford to take life as it came. Brittany's biggest problem was whether she should marry Brent, the thoracic surgeon, or Bret, the oncologist. She had life by the horns, and like few others, truly controlled her own destiny.

"Girl, with that Halle Berry cut, and that big old butt, people are going to think you got a little black in you," Mia told Brittany.

"Well, I've had some black in me before,"

Brittany laughed. "Remember Gary?"

"You're nasty!" Kim laughed.

Brittany rose and started bouncing her butt like a video girl. The three of them broke into uncontrollable laughter. Brittany seated herself and tugged at Mia's red, white, and blue Obama t-shirt.

"That is so cute!" Brittany told her.

"That's what I said!" Kim told them.

"What's your boy gonna do?" Brittany asked.

"Win!" Mia said determinedly. "He doesn't have a choice, not with Mia on his team! It's win or win, no other option."

"They are really getting down on him about changing his position on drilling offshore," Brittany told her.

"And for changing his position on opening up the national petroleum reserves," Kimberly added.

"He had to," Mia told them. "People are so blind, so short sighted. All they are worried about is how much they are paying for gas today. They don't understand that nothing can be done to change gas prices in the immediate future. We could discover an oil deposit the size of Texas, but it takes time to extract it, refine it, and distribute it. And we don't have enough refining capacity to deal with the oil being extracted now! But all they want to hear is more drilling, more oil, forget about the environmental consequences!"

"Calm down, girlfriend!" Brittany said, laughing.

"Well, you know how I get about my candidate!" Mia warned them. "Don't mess with my Obama."

"You sound like Obama girl!" Kimberly told her.

"I hope I don't see you on U-tube!" Brittany laughed.

"Can you imagine me shaking my skinny Asian ass on U-tube?" Mia said, laughing.

"Just don't get a stalking case when he shows up to campaign in New York," Kimberly added.

"Girl, speaking of crazy, how's that super ghetto boss of yours?" Mia asked.

"Crazier than ever," Kim exhaled. "Still screaming and shouting about getting her money."

Mia and Brittany laughed.

"She sounds like she should be singing the hook in a Rick Ross video!" Kim told them. "Get my money!"

"Girl, how you still there, I don't know," Brittany told her.

"It's a job," Kim exhaled. "Besides, I keep

telling myself that things will get better. She'll leave, get fired, get promoted, something will happen. It can't get worse, so it has to get better."

"What about your crazy client?" Mia asked Brittany.

"Ms. Diva, or Ms. Pencil Neck?" Brittany asked.

"Ms. Pencil Neck," Mia told her.

"Girl, I want to strangle her," Brittany told them. "She thinks that since she's with the Ford Agency now, that her shit doesn't stink. She refuses to take the jobs that I get for her as her agent, and refuses to do the promotions that I set up for her as her publicist. And she has a bad habit of making everyone around her feel fat."

Mia and Kimberly laughed.

"Girl, I know that I am not fat," Brittany told them. "Yeah, I got a booty on me, but other than that, I'm not fat. And my booty is not all flabby and fat with cellulite either."

"Girl, you are *not* fat!" Kim told her.

"Then tell me why this bitch asked me if I had to shop in the *women's* section of the department store? Brittany asked.

"No she didn't!" Mia chimed in.

"Just because her anorexic, size zero ass shops

in the junior miss section…"

The waiter arrived.

"Grand Marnier Shrimp," Kimberly told him.

"Same here," Mia added.

"Same here," Brittany told him.

The waiter nodded and disappeared.

"You better watch your weight, Brittany," Kim said jokingly.

"Girl, don't play with me," Brittany told her. "I spend all day with skinny bitches, with pouty lips, walking like their legs are broke, with people telling them all how beautiful they are. The last thing I need is to be reminded that I'm *not* a size zero!"

Kim, Mia, and Brittany broke into laughter.

"Speaking of junior miss, Brent said that he saw John at the mall the other day," Brittany announced.

"What does that have to do with junior miss?" Kimberly asked.

"Bret said that the pop tart he was with, looked young enough to be his little sister," Brittany told them.

"What?" Mia asked, leaning in.

"He said that the little girl looked about eighteen."

Kimberly exhaled and waved her hand,

dismissing the topic. "Well, another baby momma for him. Girl, I have moved on, and I wish him all the best."

"C'mon, now, Kim," Mia said. "We are your girls, and we know how much John meant to you."

"He was your fiancée," Brittany added.

"You stayed in bed for how long after you two broke up?" Mia asked.

"All water under the bridge, "Kimberly told them. "I am *so* over that man."

Mia and Brittany exchanged knowing glances.

"Yeah, sure," Mia told her.

"I am."

"Men like John don't exactly grow on trees," Brittany declared.

"You have two of them," Kim reminded her.

"Yeah, but that's only because my last name is Sherwood." Brittany told them. "I got assholes coming out of the closet, thinking that they are going to get their hands on some of my Daddy's money. Girl, I've had boyfriends that have left Ferrari brochures on the bed."

"Get out of here!" Mia said, bursting into laughter.

"Yes, I have!" Brittany shouted. "Trust me, good men don't come a dime a dozen!"

"Men are dogs!" Mia declared.

"More like animals," Kim told them.

"I agree, they are animals," Brittany said. "But some of them do make good pets,"

The three of them broke into laughter.

Kimberly exhaled. "I wonder when I'll find the right pet."

"Until then, do what I did," Mia told her.

"What's that?" Brittany asked.

"Get a tea cup poodle to keep you company during the day, and vibrator named Kong to keep you company at night."

"Bitch, you're nasty!" Brittany told her.

"Slut," Kim said, shaking her head and laughing.

Mia smiled at them. "Thank you."

Chapter Five

The meeting at K&G Men's fashions was going as expected. It was another boardroom filled with men, ogling her body. Even though she had chosen a very conservative jacket and skirt by Escada, their eyes still walked up and down her body, and their seductive smiles and suggestive whispers amongst themselves told her what they were thinking. They weren't paying attention to what she saying, only to the way her ass looked in her skirt. It was another wasted presentation.

"Gentlemen, now if you turn to page ten in the prospectus, you'll see the correlation between advertising in our magazine and the revenue growth companies have experience from it," Kimberly told them. "We have been extremely profitable for similarly situated companies. I can guarantee you that your numbers will show an increase many times over what you spend. Your ad will pay for itself in a day."

Ken, the company's vice president, leaned forward in his seat. "I compliment you on a very thorough, very persuasive, and very well done presentation. Our numbers are very positive this fiscal quarter, and our projections for next quarter are through the roof. I'm just trying to gauge how beneficial these ad dollars would be, being as though our revenue is already well into the black. There's a balance that we have to strike here, and spending money on advertisement while our numbers are so positive, might be throwing away dollars that could be well spent elsewhere."

Kimberly started to speak, but Ken held up his hand silencing her.

"I'm just having a hard time visualizing a thirty percent increase in sales, when our sales have reached an all time high at present," Ken continued, while shaking his head.

"I have a problem seeing such a bump in revenue, because your readers are primarily women, while our buyers, distributors, and consumers are almost wholeheartedly men," Kerry, the company vice president added.

She was used to this argument. "Women buy men's clothing. They make purchase decisions for their husbands, for their boyfriends, and for their sons."

"Our business suits are primarily purchased by a different demographic, Ms. Neel," Ken told her. "Our buyer's mommies don't pick their suits. We sell business attire for executives who have climbed the corporate latter to some degree."

"You are familiar with our demographics, Ms. Neel?" Kerry asked.

"Of course," Kimberly told him. "And the women who read our magazine are primarily professional women, who are married to professional men. And I do believe that you are underestimating the number of men who pick up our magazine and read through it."

Ken leaned back in his chair, exhaled, and gave Kimberly a long hard glance. The silence throughout the room was deafening, as he stared at her for what seemed to be an eternity. For the first time in a long time, Kimberly found herself becoming nervous.

"I'm inclined to give you a chance, Ms. Neel," Ken told her. "A very small chance. We'll take out a single ad, and watch the numbers the following month. If we show a bounce, and our marketing department can trace that bounce to your magazine, then you'll have yourself a full year's worth of advertisement. If not, then it was nice doing business with you."

Kimberly couldn't help the smile that crept across her face. "You won't regret it, sir."

Ken nodded, closed his prospectus, and rose from the table. "See Martin from accounting, and he'll take care of the check. Then get with Dan in marketing."

Kimberly nodded, and began to gather her presentation material. This would get Laquisha off of her back for at least a day or two. And two days without Ms. Ghetto Queen screaming that *'a bitch better have her money'*, was better than none. It would give her time to concentrate on some of the big fish that she had lined up.

*****

Kimberly left K&G Men's Fashions with a bounce in her step. Gravity seemed less weighty, and the burden on her shoulders to produce ad revenue was less heavy. She was on cloud nine and felt as though she could conquer the world. It was this new found confidence that allowed her to do something she never imagined doing; something that she had only dreamed of doing. Kimberly stopped at the large double glass doors to Vespasian's New York office, pulled them open, and strutted inside.

She had passed those doors several times throughout her career. Always on the way to or from meetings with other companies, she dreamed of the day when she could take on a meeting with the Italian giant. But for the longest, like everyone else in the marketing and advertising industry, she was deathly afraid of approaching the fashion giant. Everyone knew that Vespasian had their own powerful marketing arm. You didn't call them, *they* summoned you. They advertised when they saw fit, which was rare, because such household names didn't really need to advertise. In the world of automobiles, one rarely saw a Rolls Royce advertisement. In the world of private corporate jets, one rarely came across a Gulfstream ad. The best didn't advertise, they simply set the standards. In the world of men's business suits, Vespasian was the standard bearer. Her shaking legs told her that she had just made a humongous mistake.

"May I help you?" the receptionist asked.

"Yes, I'm here for the meeting," Kim lied. Her

voice crackled because of her nerves.

"Oh, you're late," the receptionist told her. "They've been expecting you."

The receptionist pressed a button beneath her desk, and a pair of glass sliding doors opened just behind her. "You can go into the conference room, they may still be in there."

"Thank you," Kim said, nodding and smiling. She raced through the doors not believing that she was truly in. Now, she just had to convince the company's head honchos that advertising in Mocha, was the best thing they could ever do for their company.

Kimberly crept down the hall until she came to a massive set of wooden double doors. The bronze plaque outside of the door read President, and she could hear someone in the office talking on the telephone. She exhaled, smoothed out her skirt, and pushed open the doors to find her target hanging up the telephone.

"May I help you?" Wilson asked. He removed one of Sterling's boxes from off of the desk and sat it on the floor.

Kimberly was utterly surprised to find a Black man sitting behind the president's desk, of an Italian fashion house. Perhaps he was simply in charge of the company's New York office, she thought. But nonetheless, she thought it good fortune. The brothers didn't seem to be able to keep their eyes off of her, and for the first time in her career, Kimberly decided to use all of her assets. She stuck out her chest and seductively strolled further into the office. "No, but I can help you."

Wilson lifted an eyebrow. "Oh, really? And how would you be able to help me?"

"By significantly increasing the revenues of your company," Kimberly told him.

Wilson laughed. "Really? And how would you do that? Wait a minute. Did Sterling send you here?"

"Sterling?" Kim hesitated for several moments. She had taken a chance walking into the office, bluffing her way past the receptionist, and then walking into the president's office. She was all in now, so one more lie wasn't going to hurt. "Sterling, yeah."

Wilson leaned back and propped his feet on Sterling's old desk. "Okay, let me hear it."

Kimberly opened up her brief case, and handed Wilson a generic prospectus. "Advertising in Mocha, will increase your exposure significantly, thus increasing your revenue. Vespasian has a line of women's business attire, purses, shoes, and other accessories. Reaching out to our readers and making them away of your upcoming lineups will increase your product roll out sales by a significant percent."

"And I'm sure Sterling has told you about our new expanded women's line?" Wilson asked.

"Yes," Kimberly said nervously. She wondered if he could tell that she was lying through her teeth. "That's why I'm here. Advertising your new women's line in Mocha before the launch, will result in launch sales that are through the roof."

"We were planning a roll out campaign, but I thought we were going to do it through marketing," Wilson told her. "Did Sterling say why he was bringing in outside entities?"

"No, and you're not really bringing in outside entities. I mean, I'm from Mocha. How could you launch an expanded women's line, and *not* advertise in Mocha? Mocha is the premiere women's magazine in the country."

Wilson nodded.

"So, what does he want? Does he want us to roll out the campaign immediately? It would make since to do it that way. But we haven't finalized our designs, gathered our design team, nor pulled in a

CEO to run the darn thing. Dropping an ad now would be premature. But then again, we could run with what we have finalized so far."

Kimberly nodded.

"We could start advertising our reversible, glow-in-dark, multi-color handbags and our bracelet clutches," Wilson said, thinking out loud. He reached into a box behind the desk and pulled out one of the new Vespasian multi-color handbags and tossed it to her. "Here, this is yours. You're going to have to show it to your magazine in order for them to get a preliminary idea of what we're going to advertise. Besides, I imagine you move in the same circles that we're tying to reach with our new bags, and there's nothing like a little live advertising to spark interest in a product."

Kimberly examined the bag. It was black, with gold V's. She placed her hand over the bag, and the V's glowed yellow in faint light. The purse had gold clasps and buckles, and beige leather handles. It was fierce.

"Thank you," she said stuttering.

Wilson waved her off. "Don't mention it. Look, we have some preliminary layouts from our new bags that marketing had done. You can get with Elaine over in marketing and get the layouts. Call

Natalie, set up an appointment and let us have a look at the glossies once you're done. We approve, we cut the check and run the ads. Once we get the other items finalized, we'll run some subsequent ads for the new stuff."

She didn't even have to go through her presentation, or let him salivate over her body. This was definitely her lucky day. Wilson leaned forward and lifted his telephone.

"Elaine, I'm sending…" He paused and peered up at her inquisitively.

"Kimberly."

"Kimberly," he repeated. "I'm sending Kimberly over to pick up the layouts for the new reversibles. Give her the one for the full size, the bucket, and the small bag." Wilson hung up the telephone and peered up at her. "She's waiting for you. Do you know how to get to marketing?"

Kimberly shrugged.

"It's four floors down."

"Got it," Kim said, gathering her materials. Another one bites the dust, she thought excitedly as she headed out of the office. Her check was going to be *fat* next month.

The trip out of the office and to the elevator was a quick one. Kimberly found herself waiting at one of the many lifts in the center of the Empire State Building. She was anxious to get to marketing and then get back to her office and get the photos to her layout department. The faster things moved, the quicker she could show Vespasian's head honchos the layout, and the quicker she could get that check from their accounting department.

"Hi," Sterling said breathing heavily. He sat the boxes that he was carrying on the ground.

"Hi," Kimberly replied. He was cute, she thought. Sexy, low cut hair, well groomed, well dressed.

"Nice purse," he said with a smile.

Kimberly held up the new Vespasian hand bag. "Thanks."

"You always carry two of them?" he asked, shifting between her Dooney and Burke bag, and her new Vespasian one.

"No, not really," she said, smiling. She lifted the Vespasian handbag. "It was a gift."

"Nice gift," he told her. "Wow, those haven't even hit the market yet."

"I know." Kim paused and then turned toward him. "But how do you know that? Are you one of those metro sexual males that keep up with all the latest fashions?"

"Actually, I don't consider myself to be one of those metro sexual males, but I do keep up with all the latest fashion trends," Sterling replied. "It's kinda my job to do that."

"Oh, really?"

Sterling kicked at the boxes next to his feet. Kimberly peered down at the labels on the boxes. Vespasian was stenciled across them in giant letters.

"Oh, you work for Vespasian?" Kim said, surprised.

Sterling nodded.

"What do you do there?" Kim asked.

"Everything. Right now, I cleaning out a junky office, and carrying boxes down to the compactor."

Kim nodded and smiled.

"So, what do you do, Ms…"

"Kimberly," she told him, extending her hand.

"Sterling," he replied, gently clasping her hand and shaking it. "Pleased to meet you, Kimberly."

"Likewise. And my friends call me Kim."

"Lucky them."

"Why is that?"

"Because they know you well enough to call you Kim. I envy them."

"Don't," she said with a smile. "You can call

me Kim too."

"So, I'm considered a friend?" Sterling asked, lifting an eyebrow.

"For right now."

The elevator door opened, and Sterling lifted his boxes and followed Kimberly on board.

"So, can I really *call* you, Kim?"

"You can call me Kim."

"No, I think you misunderstood me," Sterling smiled. "I was asking if I could really *call you*, Kim."

"Ahhh," she said blushing. "Smooth."

Sterling laughed.

"I don't know about you just yet," Kim told him.

Sterling turned his palms up. "What's there to know?"

The elevator door opened, and Kimberly stepped off of the lift, and turned back toward Sterling. "You're a little to smooth and sexy to get my number off the top, Mr. Man. Maybe after I check up on you on little bit."

Sterling smiled and nodded, just as the elevator door slid to a close. She was the nicest sister he had come across in a long time. Dressed to kill, sexy green eyes, fierce hair cut, immaculate body, great personality, wonderful sense of humor; she was the entire package. Sterling silently hoped that he would run into her again, and that she had done her checking up. He definitely wanted to get to know her and be counted amongst her friends.

Chapter Six

One would expect a restaurant like Ms. Emma's to be located in Harlem, or Brooklyn, and even Queens for that matter. But the fact of the matter, was that the city's premiere soul food restaurant, was located smack dab in the middle of Manhattan.

Ms. Emma's was an award-winning soul food delight that attracted all of the city's superstars and movers and shakers. Ms. Emma herself still ran the place, and even in some cases, personally prepared the meals. She had been in the same location for thirty years, and had for the most part, maintained the same neo soul décor for most of that time. But it wasn't the décor that kept bringing patrons back, it was the food. No one this side of the Mason Dixon line fried chicken the way Ms. Emma did. It had just the right crispness on the outside, and was tender and juicy on the inside. And her secret herbs and spices made the chicken taste like it fell from above. Ms. Emma's was one of the crew's favorite meeting places for their Wednesday get-togethers.

"He was finer than a strand of silk, girl!" Kimberly told them. "He smelled so good, and so clean; almost like eucalyptus mixed with baby lotion. And he had this goatee and haircut that looked like he just got up out of the barber's chair."

Mia and Brittany squealed.

Mia clasped Kimberly's forearm. "I can't believe you!"

"Girl, he was fine!" Kim continued. "He had this nice, Vespasian suit on, that looked as if it had been tailored just for him. And he had this wonderful charm about him."

"I can't believe that you didn't give him your telephone number!" Brittany told her.

"I know," Kim told them. "Trust me, I've been kicking myself in the foot ever since."

"Girl, is this a John thing?" Mia asked.

"A John thing?" Kim repeated, lifting an inquisitive eyebrow.

"Yeah, one of those things where you're afraid to move on, just in case you and the ex might get back together," Mia explained.

"You can't just sit around crying over spilled milk," Brittany told her.

"Yeah," Mia added. "Sitting around waiting for John to come back is not healthy."

"I'm not waiting for John!" Kimberly protested.

"He was Mr. Right," Mia told her. "But he was Mr. Right for Somebody Else. He wasn't the one, Kim."

"I know," Kimberly said softly.

"Don't block your chances with someone else, because you're stuck in the past." Mia told her.

"I know," Kimberly nodded. "I won't."

"Next super sexy man you come across who is interested in you, you pass him those digits," Brittany told her.

Kim nodded. "Deal."

"Deal," Mia concurred.

"Deal," Brittany said, joining in.

Kimberly peered down at her watch. "Got to go. Have that meeting at the dealership." Kimberly opened her purse and pulled out her wallet.

"Girl, please!" Brittany told her. "Lunch is on Daddy." Brittany produced a black American Express Card, causing them all to burst into laughter.

"I love that purse," Mia declared, lifting Kimberly's new Vespasian purse into the air. "I can't believe they just gave it to you."

"This thing already has a waiting list," Brittany told them. "Even at thirty-eight hundred bucks, it has a six month waiting list already."

"And Ms. Lucky, here, just had one tossed into her lap!" Mia said, poking Kim in the arm. "I am so jealous!"

"Well, let's just hope my luck continues!" Kim told them, rising from the table.

"Good luck to you," Brittany told her.

"Knock 'em dead!" Mia told her.

"See you girls later!" Kim said, waving and heading off for her meeting.

*****

The dealership was one of the largest and most successful Mercedes Benz dealerships in the country. They not only sold cars throughout the New York metropolitan area, but throughout the nation, thanks to e-Bay Motors, DuPont, and other online ventures. Advertising in Mocha would not only increase their exposure in the African American market on the East Coast, but nationwide as well. Going after the dollars of well to do African American women made sense for the dealership, and so they were very interested in hearing what Mocha Magazine had to offer. And so, Kimberly was about to give her presentation to an already receptive General Manager. The sale was practically in the bag, all she had to do was not blow it.

"John…" Kimberly stuttered.

Dr. Johnathan Vasser turned and spied his ex fiancé standing just behind him. He opened his arms wide and pulled her into his embrace. "Kimberly!"

"John…"

"How wonderful to see you!" John told her. "How have you been?"

"Good," Kim said, swallowing hard. "I've been fine. How about you? How have you been?"

"Wonderful," he smiled. "I finally opened my own practice. After talking about it for years, I finally made the plunge."

Kimberly nodded. "That's great news. I always knew that you had it in you."

"You gave me the courage to do it," he told

her. "You always made me a stronger, better, wiser person."

Kimberly felt herself slowly melting. He looked like a chocolate Adonis, clothed in a tailored Armani suit. The man had it all. Perfect teeth, perfect hair, perfect skin, perfect breath, perfect cologne, perfect education, perfect job, perfect breeding, perfect house, perfect car, perfect *everything*. He just needed to either wrap his weenie up tighter, or get a vasectomy. Three kids, by three different women, had been too much for her. Especially when those baby mommas all still wanted to be Mrs. Vasser, and when he did little to control them or put them in check. He was the perfect man, with way to much drama in his life. And drama, was something she *desperately* wanted to steer clear of.

"What are you doing here?" Kimberly asked.

John waved his hand around the showroom. "It's obvious, I'm shopping for a vehicle."

"Another one?" Kimberly smiled. "What, you want one for each day of the week?"

John laughed heartily. "No, actually, this one is for a friend. A really close friend."

"You're buying cars for friends now?" Kimberly asked with a raised eyebrow.

"Actually, it's kind of an engagement gift."

"Wow, what a wonderful gift. You must be very close to the happy couple."

John exhaled and broke down. "Okay, it's for my fiancée. It's an engagement gift for my fiancée."

"Get out of here!" Kimberly told him. The news hit her in her gut like a ton of bricks. "Congratulations!"

Kim leaned forward and hugged John once again. "Who's the lucky girl?"

John shook his head. "You don't know her. She's from upstate."

"Oh, well. I can't wait to meet her."

"You and your parents are on the guest list. Invitations go out next week I believe."

"Well, thank you." Kimberly turned toward a one hundred and twenty thousand dollar S550 SL. It was a two seat convertible, red with a tan leather interior. "I think this is the one."

John peered down at the convertible and nodded. "You're right. I think I'll take it."

A suited gentleman walked from the rear of the dealership and approached her.

"Ms. Neel, I'm Red McCreedy, General Manager," the gentlemen said, extending his hand toward her.

"A pleasure," Kimberly told him, while shaking his hand.

The general manager waved his hand toward a nearby hallway. "My office is this way. We can sit down and go over your information."

"Thank you," Kimberly said, starting off. She stopped, and turned back toward John. "It was nice running into you again. You look real good. Congratulations, and you give my best wishes to that lucky bride to be."

John nodded, and watched as she headed down the hall with the general manager of the dealership.

"Please, have a seat," McCreedy told her, waving toward a chair in front of his desk.

Kim seated herself. She was shaking visibly.

"Are you okay?" McCreedy asked.

"Yes," Kim said, her voice cracking. She lifted her leather portfolio with her shaking hands, and accidentally spilled its contents all over the floor. "I'm so sorry."

"That's okay," McCreedy told her. "Can I get you some coffee or something?"

Kimberly's hands moved uncontrollably all over her body. She touched her face, fiddled with her blouse, rubbed her skirt, and looked completely discombobulated. Seeing John had totally flustered her. And the news of his engagement had hit her hard. The thought of him laying with another woman, loving another woman, being intimate with another woman disturbed her greatly. She never thought that she could truly love another, and the thought that he could, truly disturbed her. Despite her denials to her family and friends, John was hers. He was her soul mate. Deep down, she had hoped and prayed each night that he would get himself together and commit to their relationship. All he needed to do, was tell his ex's to back off; To stand up for her and for their relationship. He just needed to be a man, and tell them that he was with *her* now, and that was that. He needed to tell them that he would take care of his children, but all of the extracurricular drama was over with. But instead of doing those things, he had simply moved on. Now, he was marrying some young tart from upstate. How had it all come to this, she wondered?

McCreedy handed Kim a cup of water. "What's the matter? Are you diabetic or something? You're shaking like a leaf?"

"I'm sorry," Kim said, gathering her materials. "Can we reschedule this?"

"Sure," he nodded. "I don't know when I'll have another opening in my schedule."

"I'm sorry." Kimberly rose. "I'll give you a call."

McCreedy stood behind his desk, and watched as she rushed out of the dealership.

Chapter Seven

Sterling lifted his iron and swung with a force that would have made Tiger Woods envious. The tiny golf ball was sent flying across the grass-tee driving range of the practice facility, landing very near the limit of the facility's edge. The driving range was a part of the Upper Montclair Country Club's state-of-the-art practice facility. It was a facility that included not only a 300 yard driving range, but a putting green, a chipping green, and sand bunkers. Nothing was too good for the country club's members, many of whom were the crème de la crème of East Coast society.

The Upper Montclair Country Club was one of those blue blood facilities that had been established at the turn of the twentieth century. It dated back to 1901, while its clubhouse dated back to the 1920's.

It boasted several dining facilities, each tailored to its various member's mood and requirements. There was a banquet room that could seat one hundred and eighty people, a club room for casual dining, a member's grille for less formal dining, a terrace for dining al fresco, a West lounge for more intimate dining, and a traveler's room for business luncheons or private dining. But what Sterling loved most about the facility, was its golf course.

The course was a 27 hole affair, designed by none other than Robert Trent Jones Sr. It was immaculately maintained, while the service, amenities, and pro shop were something that could only be experienced. It seemed as though the facility anticipated its patron's needs, even before the patron's could express them. It was this service, and the facility's convenient location to his Montville, New Jersey estate, that kept him coming back.

"Man, you should have seen her," Sterling told Wilson. "Yellow bone, with skin like buttermilk. Green eyes, a sexy pixie haircut, nice up top, thick hips, and butt that you could sit a coffee cup on!"

Wilson and Sterling broke into laughter.

"I mean, baby girl was fine with a capital F," Sterling continued. "And she had it all together.

She was witty, charming, and she had this sexy confidence about her."

Wilson snapped his fingers. "Wait a minute, are you talking about the one you sent to the office the other day?"

Sterling shook his head. "I didn't send anyone to the office. Especially anyone that looked like that!"

"I could have swore she said that you sent her," Wilson said. He paused for a moment, and then shrugged his shoulders. "Oh well. Anyway, it's good to hear you talk about a women with so much passion again. I never thought that I'd hear you so excited about another women, not after Carmela."

This time Sterling shrugged. "I never thought I'd be like this either, but baby girl had it going on."

"And she wouldn't give you the digits?" Wilson smiled and shook his head. "You need some help from the master?"

"The master?" Sterling swung his club once again, and sent another golf ball flying down range. "Please! You couldn't catch a cold if you walked across Alaska naked and dripping wet."

"Sterling, do I have to take you to the club and prove it to you *again*?" Wilson asked, lifting an eyebrow.

"I don't do the club thing anymore, and that's good for you, or else I would have to take you up on that bet."

"Bloomingdales, Neiman Marcus, Saks, Walmart, you name the place!" Wilson said excitedly. "The teacher will take you to school!"

Sterling and Wilson laughed heartily.

"Will, you're crazy," Sterling said, concentrating on his swing once again.

"So how do you plan on finding this mystery lady?" Wilson asked.

Sterling shrugged his shoulders. "I don't know. She said that she worked for Mocha. Maybe I could have someone do a little checking around."

"Mocha, Mocha, Mocha, hmmm." Wilson lifted an eyebrow. "I could have sworn that sister that came to my office said that she worked for Mocha. But I could have sworn that you sent her. How else could she have gotten past security? This is weird. In fact, I believe I gave her a purse."

Sterling peered up from his practice. "She definitely had one of our handbags, but I didn't send her. Are you sure she said that *I* sent her?"

"I believe so," Wilson said, shaking his head. "But then again, I don't remember. I've been seeing dozens of people the last few days, searching for models for the upcoming fashion event in The Hamptons, interviewing designers, and interviewing executives to run the line, as well as dozens of other people for various positions around the company. I just don't remember."

Sterling waved him off. "Ahhh, don't worry about it. If it was meant to be, I'll run into her again."

*****

"I don't understand what the fuck this bitch is trying to say!" Laquisha shouted, throwing the fax from the corporate office across the room. "Them bitches in Atlanta gots me all fucked up! AOL Time Warner can kiss the blackest part of my ass! *Kimberly, Jerome, Pamela, Aisha,* and *Lani,* get y'all asses in here!"

The group filtered into the office one by one.

"Take y'all time," Laquisha told them.

The group seated themselves in various chairs arrayed around the office.

"First off, what the hell is this?" Laquisha

asked, tossing some papers to Lani. "This is supposed to be a tug-at-your-heart piece about Haitian immigrants coming across the water in shoddy makeshift life rafts. Instead, I get a technical piece about immigration and the courts, and the legal challenges facing the Haitian immigrants. Try again."

Laquisha wheeled, and turned toward Aisha. "And you! You're supposed to be my fashion writer, but the only articles you've been sending me, have been dealing with the *business* of fashion, and not the clothing itself! I know you want to move over to what you consider more serious writer pursuits, but for right now, you work for Mocha as a *fashion* writer. So write about some damn fashion!"

"And you!" Laquisha shouted, turning toward Kimberly. "Why I get a call from the Benz dealership, asking if your ass was alright? What the hell is wrong with you? What did you go down there and pull? You were too sick to close a deal that was basically in the bag? I'll bet your ass won't be too sick to walk in here and pick up your damn paycheck on Friday, will you? This is some straight up bullshit!"

"And you!" she shouted, turning toward Jerome. "Your little fairy ass fucked up my Army contract, flirting with the fucking ad specialist! They requested that I send someone else!"

"Someone else!" Jerome shouted. "That bastard! He didn't want someone else when he was trying to get into my panties!"

"*Drawers*, Jerome!" Laquisha shouted. "You wear *fucking drawers*! You're a *man*!"

Jerome shrugged. "I wouldn't bet on it."

Laquisha through her pen up in the air and rolled her eyes. "Why did I walk into that one?"

"What did I do?" Pamela asked.

"Actually, nothing," Laquisha told her. "But I just didn't want you to feel left out. Since I have nothing to yell at you about, I'll just say this. Keep on getting my paper!"

Laquisha ran her hand across her sweaty brow, clearing away the perspiration that she had worked up. She drew in a deep breath, calming herself before continuing. "Now, the reason I called you all in here, is because I have to send some of you to the fashion show in The Hamptons this weekend. Naturally, I'm going to send my *least* fucked up people. Pam, you and Kim go and work the crowd for accounts, and Lani and Aisha, you go and cover the show for the magazine. I'm sending Pezo to take the photographs for us. His shots, plus whatever we're able to buy from the freelancers should cover us pretty good."

"Are we staying in The Hamptons?" Kimberly asked.

"What do you mean?" Laquisha asked.

"Is Mocha paying for us to stay in The Hamptons?" Kimberly clarified.

"Is the Pope Baptist?" Laquisha cackled. "Hell no, Mocha ain't paying for you to stay in the damn Hamptons.

"Why can't I go?" Jerome pleaded.

"Because you're on my shit list right now!" Laquisha shouted. "Look, I want some good shit outta this weekend. I want great photos, fantastic stories, and a lot of fucking ad sales. Do y'all got that?"

Nods went around the room.

"Traditionally, this show has been a big producer for us, and it's always given us a boost in magazine sales," Laquisha told them. "I want that tradition to continue. So let's get out there and get it done."

"Laquisha, one question," Lani said, rising from her seat.

"Yeah?"

"What kinda human interest story am I going

84

to get from The Hampton's fashion show?"

"I don't know, you're the writer, you think of something!" Laquisha shouted. "Maybe some skinny model bitch breaks her nail and believes that her career is in ruins."

"I got the perfect stories for you," Aisha told Lani. "You can do designer profiles, chronicling their struggles to make it in the industry. I can hook you up with some of the designers."

"That's what I like to hear!" Laquisha told them. "You bitches work together and get my money!"

Just Another Damn Love Story

Chapter Eight

The Hamptons were known for its collection of high dollar mansions, star filled social season, and mind blowing celebrity parties. It was also known for its yachting regalia, its charity events, and its star studded fashion shows. This year's biggest show, was being held at Guild Hall, a restored five-acre estate in East Hampton Point. All of the industry's movers and shakers would be there.

This year's theme was Feng Shui, the ancient Chinese art and science for protection and good fortune. None other than Eric Clapton, Chris Brown, and Mary J. Blige, would be performing the first night, while Elton John, Keisha Cole, Lauren Hill, and Goapele would take center stage the second night. Wyclef Jean, George Straight, Rhianna, and Usher, would close out the third night with a bang. This year's event was being sponsored by Imani Cosmetics, Bobbi Brown Cosmetics,

Mercedes Benz, and Tanqueray.

The sponsors had spent huge sums turning Guild Hall and its corresponding acreage into a beautiful Chinese botanical paradise. Ponds had been constructed, and Chinese lanterns, vases, and screens had been placed throughout the estate. And it was all done in white.

"Gianna, your designs are off the hook!" Sterling said excitedly.

"Thank you, sir," Gianna said, bowing slightly. She was Vespasian's in house designer from Milan. And she had designed this year's premiere exhibits for the design house.

"I don't know how you pulled it off," Sterling told her. "But you and Amerigo nailed this year's theme to the tee. When the other designers see what we have this year, they'll be filled with envy."

Amerigo bowed his head in modesty. He too, was one of Vespasian's hot young Sicilian designers, working out of the company's Milan office. He had nailed the white, cotton, double breasted men's suits that Vespasian would be showcasing. The suits were reminiscent of the fine Italian suits worn by the famous Chicago and New York gangsters during prohibition. They were the same suits worn by the Japanese Yakuza, and Chinese mafiosos, and thus gave Vespasian the theme for their men's line. They gave the white diamond suits, porcelain pin stripes, offsetting the base color just enough to be seen by the naked eye. They put Tommy guns in the hands of their male models, put them in some porcelain colored gators, some white diamond fedoras, and placed some fat Cuban cigars in their mouths. Vespasian also brought in some white diamond colored, nineteen twenty Lincoln Continentals for their models to ride in on. And they made sure that all of their models were Chinese. They were going to show out this season.

As wonderful as the men's line was, the women's line was going to be even better. Gianna had paired a white pearl Kimono type dress with flowing butterfly sleeves, with a pair of white pearl espadrilles with six inch wedges. The white pearl dresses had white porcelain colored dragons flowing over them, as well as the Chinese characters for Feng Shui. Her Chinese models also carried white silk umbrellas, with white bamboo handles that matched the dresses. Their faces were painted white, and made up in the style of the Geisha. Sterling said that she had showed her ass off with this first design.

Gianna's second showing, was a strapless

white Georgette style dress with flowing butterfly sleeves and a flowing and layered butterfly hem. The dress had gold V's printed over it, and was paired with some T strap chain sandals, that had gold Vespasian V's as the chains. The look was East meets West; a pairing of Beijing and Milan, uniting the best of both worlds.

Gina's third showing, was a white form fitting dress, with a sweetheart neckline, that she paired with a breathtaking pair of quarter-calf, leg-wrap sandals. The sandals, whose tiny white straps wrapped themselves up to a quarter of the wearer's calf, were show stealers. The crowd couldn't stop the gasping, and then clapping and cheering after seeing them.

And Sterling went all out with his last showing. He chose to have Rick Ross's song 'Boss' blasted on the loudspeaker when the model strutted out onto the stage. She wore a white, oversized, rabbit fur, hooded parka, with rabbit feet sewn the length of it, serving as the toggles. It fit right in with this year's motif of good fortune. This year, even Donatella had to bow down and give him his props.

"Okay, you showed your ass, this year," Kimberly told him.

Sterling turned in her direction. "Hello!" He was surprised out of this world.

"Allow me to introduce my friends and colleagues, Pamela Winslow, and Aisha Green," Kimberly told him.

"Please to meet you," Sterling told them, shaking each of their hands in turn.

"Kim said that you work for Vespasian," Pam said nodding. "I have to admit, you guys stole the show this year."

"That white Kimono was off the chain!" Aisha told him. "And that model, with her teeny-tiny feet in those high ass wedges, she looked just like a damn Geisha! You guys are off the charts this year!"

"What exactly do you do for Vespasian, Sterling?" Pam asked.

"Everything!" Sterling said laughing.

"He's right, I saw him carrying boxes," Kimberly said laughing.

"Oh, so you're just like us," Aisha said. "A jack of all trades, but under appreciated by all the higher ups."

The ladies all lifted their glasses in a toast.

"To the under appreciated!" Kim said. "The ones that make the company go round and round."

"But who get stepped on!" Pam added.

"And who get the shitty assignments, and the worst pay!" Aisha added.

"This is not exactly a shitty assignment," Sterling said, waving his hand around at the beautiful set up.

"No, not this one," Pam agreed. "But wait until you're on that plane flying coach."

"With that hollering baby in the seat across the aisle," Kim said, shaking her head.

"And that bad ass little boy behind you, kicking the back of your seat," Aisha added.

"And that fly mouth, flippant stewardess who looks down on you because you're flying coach!" Kimberly said.

"And the cheap motel room, the funky crowds of journalists, the…" Aisha started.

Sterling held up his hands. "Okay, okay, I get you."

Aisha pulled out a tiny digital recorder. "So, can I interview you?"

"Are you somebody worth interviewing, Sterling?" Pamela asked.

Sterling laughed. "That depends on who you ask."

"Okay, okay, I'm not going to let y'all torture

my friend," Kim told her friends. She interlaced her arms with Sterling's and led off. The two of them slowly made their way through the crowd, toward the pier.

"So, are you here on assignment?" Sterling asked.

"Something like that," Kim replied.

"So, what exactly do you do for Mocha?"

"I'm an ad executive."

"Oh, that explains it."

"Explains what?"

"Why you were in the building that day, and why you're at this fashion event today," Sterling explained. "You're lining up advertisers for your magazine."

"Correct." Kim said nodding. "And you're here because?"

"Working for Vespasian, helping out with the fashion show, making sure everything goes right."

"Okay, so what exactly do you do for them?" Kim asked.

"Everything."

"Everything," Kimberly laughed. "There goes that answer again. You're real mysterious, you know that?"

"I'm not trying to be," Sterling smiled. "In

fact, I really want you to get to know me a lot better."

"Really?" Kimberly said, lifting an eyebrow.

Sterling nodded. "Really. You running off without giving me your telephone number was torture."

"Torture?"

"Torture," Sterling confirmed. "I couldn't sleep at night, I couldn't eat. All I could do was think of you. Your smile haunted my thoughts and dreams, all day and all night."

"Oh, you're good," Kim told him. "You're a charmer. I don't give my number to guys as smooth as you."

"I get penalized for telling the truth?" Sterling asked. "I put it on everything, I thought about you a lot since that day on the elevator."

"Why?"

"Because it's not everyday that one comes across a sister so beautiful, so charming, so intelligent, so well together as yourself. You're a very memorable person. A person who I would really love to get to know a lot better."

Kimberly swallowed hard. She found herself staring into this man's hazel eyes and almost melting. He was definitely a charmer. Smooth as silk, with a voice that had her feeling moist in places that shouldn't be feeling moist. The two of them approached the pier and peered out over the yacht filled waters.

"Wow, what do you think one of these runs?" Kimberly asked.

"That one, about fifteen million."

"Wouldn't that be nice to have," she said softly. "I would live on it, and just sail around the world. The only time I would stop, would be for food and fuel, and maybe to walk on an occasional beach, or to take in an occasional sunset."

"You should never turn down the opportunity to take in a sunset," Sterling said, leaning forward and whispering into her ear. He caressed the side of her face, and gently touched his lips against hers. "Especially, if you have the opportunity to watch the sun's reflection in the eyes of someone as beautiful as yourself. You should see the sun radiating off of your skin right now."

Kimberly leaned forward and pressed her lips against Sterling's, kissing him softly at first, and then more firmly the second time. On the third kiss, their tongues met. He tasted like cinnamon to her, while she tasted like mint to him. She became lost in his embrace, and felt herself floating away.

"Don't do this to me," Kimberly whispered.

"Do what?" Sterling asked.

"This. Don't do this."

"You're going to have to explain to me what you're talking about," Sterling told her.

"What is this? What are we doing, Sterling?" Kimberly turned away from him, and peered out toward the ocean. "I'm not ready for another one of these. I can't afford to go through another one of these. Not right now, not yet."

Sterling rested him hands on her shoulders. "Afford another what? I'm not asking you to invest in anything that you don't feel you're ready for. We can take our time, be friends, get to know one another. I'm willing to go as slow as I have to, I'm willing to walk with you until the end of time, if that's what it takes."

She turned back towards him. "Why? Why are you willing to commit that type of time? You hardly know me. Am I your investment on the side, while you fulfill your needs elsewhere?"

Sterling let out a half laugh. "You give me too much credit. I don't have another woman, and I'm not in a relationship right now. I don't sleep around, and that's for two reasons. One, because my Momma raised me right, and two, because I'm afraid of HIV. I'm willing to put the time into this relationship because that's what commitment is all about. You're worth it, Kimberly, and whoever led you to believe that you weren't worth a man's full commitment has you fooled. You're an extraordinary woman, and I'm glad that I met you."

Kimberly reached into her purse, pulled out her business card, and handed it to Sterling. "My cell phone number is on there also."

Sterling smiled and tucked the card into his pocket. "Thank you."

"No, thank you, Sterling," Kim told him. "I haven't had a man make me feel like that in some time."

"Feel like what?"

"Worthy."

"Sterling!" A voice called out to him from behind.

Sterling and Kimberly turned in the direction from which it came.

"I just had to come and shake your hand personally." The gentleman told him.

"Sergio!" Sterling said surprised.

Another gentleman walked just behind Sergio. He kissed Sterling on both cheeks.

"Georgio!" Sterling said, greeting him.

"*Bellisimo*!" Georgio declared. "You stole the show, my friend!"

"That kimono was exquisite!" Sergio told him. "And those shoes!"

"And that parka!" Georgio said, kissing the tips of his fingers. "Marvelous!"

"Well, Georgio, you and Sergio inspire me," Sterling told them.

Kimberly backed up and turned toward the ocean. Her mind was on Sterling. Could he really be all that he was cracked up to be? He seemed like a nice guy. In fact, *too* nice. That brought two questions into her head. One, was he just a big sham? Or, was he too nice for her to risk hurting? She had heard about those rebound relationships. The ones where the next guy comes along, picks you up off of your feet, and then ends up getting hurt once you're feeling better and ready to move on. Could she hurt him like that? And what about John? A man that she had loved with every fiber of her being. What if he came to her and said that he loved her, and wanted to be with her, and that he was willing to move away with her and start life fresh somewhere else? What would that mean? Would she go? Could she hurt this man standing behind her like that?

Kimberly stood facing the ocean, lost in her thoughts so much, that she never realized that she had three of the biggest designers in the world standing behind her talking.

Just Another Damn Love Story

Chapter Nine

St. Phillip's Episcopal Church was a one hundred and ninety year old neo-gothic style church, planted in the middle of Harlem's West 134th Street. It was home to the city's African American movers and shakers, and had been for most of its nearly two hundred year old existence. The Church's history read like a history book, as it had bore witness to most of the nation's great events. It even had plenty of history of its own.

The current building had been constructed in 1910, and had been designed by the first African American licensed as an architect in the State of New York. The building had been designated as a New York City designated landmark, and during the 1950's, was home to the largest Christian congregation in the United States. Such proud history is what kept the church so prominent in the eyes of the east coast's wealthy African American community. It's what kept the church's membership swollen, and what kept its coffers full. It's also what kept the wealthy Westchester crowd driving into the city for Sunday service; including the Neels.

"Glad you could make it this Sunday, darling," Marjorie Neel told her daughter.

Kimberly exhaled forcibly, and plopped down on the pew next to her mother. "Mom, don't start."

"Why, were you out late last night sinning, in that big giant nest of sin you call the city?" Marjorie asked.

Kimberly leaned forward, peering around her mother. "Hi, Dad."

"Hi, baby," Thornton Neel greeted his daughter. "Good to see you. You look really pretty today."

"Thanks, Daddy," Kim smiled. She could always count on her father to make her feel good.

Marjorie struck her husband with her church fan. "She does *not* look good, she looks tired. Tired, and thin, and exhausted from that dead end job of hers."

"Mother, we're in church," Kim whispered. "Can we not have this discussion right now?"

"Church is the best place to discuss that sinful place you live in," Marjorie continued. "Who ever heard of living in Times Square?"

"Marjorie…" Thornton said, trying to hush his wife.

"Really," Marjorie pressed on. "She should move back to Purchase."

"I can't move back in with you," Kimberly whispered.

"Not with us. You can get your own place."

"And have to commute for thirty minutes to an hour twice a day? No thank you."

"You always were a stubborn child," Marjorie huffed. "Now I see why John left you."

"John didn't leave me, Mother," Kim said sternly. "I left him."

"Another bad decision," Marjorie countered. "He's getting married, did you know that?"

"Yes, I know it," Kim whispered. "And good for him."

"That could have been you walking down that aisle," Marjorie told her. "You could have been the wife of a doctor."

"What makes you think that I want to be a doctor's wife?" Kimberly asked. "Or anybody's wife for that matter? Mother, it's the twenty first century."

Marjorie gasped. She turned toward her

husband. "Did you hear that, Thornton? Did you? This is what happens when you send your children off the National Cathedral School in D.C. to be educated. They come back as liberal lesbians."

Kimberly gasped. "Mother! I am *not* a lesbian," she said under her breath.

"What is wrong with marriage?" Marjorie asked. "Marriage to a good and descent man like John?"

"There's nothing wrong with marriage to a good and descent man, I just have to find one first. John isn't it."

"You know, your sister wouldn't have thrown him away like that. She knows what to do with a doctor."

"I'm sure she does," Kim said sarcastically.

"And what's that supposed to mean?" Marjorie asked. "Your sister and her fiancée, Dr. Giddings, are very happy. He may only be an OB-GYN, but at least that's something. He'll have his own practice one day, and they'll be very comfortable."

"And I'm happy for them," Kim whispered. "But what's good for her, isn't necessarily good for me."

"You difficult difficult child you!" Marjorie

said.

"I'm an adult now, Mom."

"Adults make adult decisions. They don't walk away from good relationships at the first sign of a little trouble."

"They broke my windows out of the Porsche you and Daddy bought me!" Kimberly said under her breath. "Another one of his ex's, spray painted my car, while another one keyed my door! I had to deal with the phone calls, the death threats, and all the other drama."

Marjorie exhaled and waved her hand, dismissing her daughter. "Come, it's almost time for the choir. Let's go and put on our choir robes. You do still sing for the Lord, don't you?"

"Of course, Mother," Kim said rising, and following her mother back into the choir room.

*****

The Visionaire was unlike any other apartment building in the world. The massive mirror glass structure had been designed by none other than world renowned architect Rafael Pelli. Not only was the design of the wedge shape building breathtaking to behold, but the building's surroundings were equally impressive. Nestled on the tip of Battery Park City, the building held a commanding view of neighboring Battery Park, the Hudson River, the Manhattan skyline, and The Statue of Liberty. Those lucky enough to live in the building were gifted with some of the most incredible views the city had to offer.

The Visionaire's lobby greeted visitors with massive stone columns, and a giant twelve foot aquarium filled with exotic tropical fish. A lounge just off of the lobby, provided guest with a pool table, a massive plasma T.V., a giant natural gas fireplace, and even a separate movie screening room.

Resident's were spoiled with a sky lit indoor swimming pool and hot tub that looked out onto one of two roof gardens, while work out buffs could pass the time away in the fitness center, which was filled with state of the art cardio and weight equipment. The world class fitness center also boasted of a spa, a sauna, a steam room, a massage room, a yoga room, and an aerobics room. And for those who wanted to relax on a more leisurely scale, the building's rooftop garden held a view of the

Hudson River. This rooftop paradise also came equipped with an outdoor events area, with built in grills and individual cabanas in case the residents wanted to do a little entertaining.

As stunning as the building itself was, the apartments were even more breathtaking. Bamboo floors greeted the guest upon entry, and continued into the kitchen where they were joined by beautifully crafted bamboo cabinets and black granite counter tops. The bamboo floors stopped only at the bathrooms, where limestone floors took their place. The luxurious affairs that were the bathrooms, boasted of teak cabinetry, marble jetted tubs, and hand crafted marble vanities. To live in the Visionaire is to have made it big time. Or, to have been born with rich parents.

"Brittany, I love your apartment!" Mia screamed once again. She peered out of the massive floor to ceiling windows, taking in the views of the Hudson and the lights beyond. "This view is breathtaking!"

"Yeah, except when it's lightening," Brittany told her.

"Brit, you're still scared of lightening?" Mia said shocked. "I thought that you were over that?"

"How?" Brittany asked, turning up her palms.

"It's a phobia. It's called Astraphobia. I'll never get over it."

"People get over their phobias all the time," Mia said.

"Duh, the reason it's called a phobia, is because it's an irrational fear," Brittany said slurring.

She and Mia broke into alcohol induced laughter.

"You guys, this is supposed to be about me!" Kim said, slurring her words.

Brittany climbed onto her crème colored leather sectional with Kim, and pulled her close. "I'm sorry. It *is* about you."

Mia joined them.

"I had to put up with an entire Sunday service of nothing but nagging from my mother," Kim told them. "Marriage, marriage, marriage, nothing but marriage. I should have married John. That could have been me walking down the aisle. Your sister is so happy. Your job really sucks. You know what, Mom? You're right, my job *does* suck!"

"That's right, just let it all out!" Mia told her.

"Why do people feel you have to be married to be happy?" Kimberly asked.

"I get it from my mom all the time," Brittany

told her.

"I don't," Mia smiled. "My mom would have a heart attack if I told her that I was going to marry Shaun."

"Why?" Brittany asked. "Shaun's cool. He's a great guy, nice looking, great job, and he treats you like a princess."

"Guys, my parents are from a different era," Mia said, wiping away a tear. "They like Shaun, but not the fact that he's Black."

"Wow!" Brittany gasped, and reached for her drink.

"Parents!" Kim shouted. "Why come they won't just let us live our lives!"

"Here, here!" Brittany said, lifting her glass in toast.

The girls held up their glasses and clinked them together.

"John, John, John! I'm so tired of hearing about John!" Kim shouted. "She thinks that John was all that! Well, he wasn't! He was a cheat, and he was weak, and he let those women dominate him!"

"A cheat?" Mia asked, lifting an eyebrow. "You think he cheated on you?"

"I know he did!" Kim told them. "All of

those late night phone calls, and him creeping off in the middle of the night. Besides that, why would all his ex's still be so hung up on him? He had to be telling them something, or giving them some reason to think that he was still going to be with them."

"Wow!" Brittany said, taking another massive drink from her glass.

"I just want to move on with my life," Kim sniffled. A tear rolled down her cheek. "Why won't my mother let me? Why won't life let me move on? I just want to be happy, what's wrong with that? I go to church, I pay my tides, I sing in the choir, I don't cheat, or steal, or kill, or hurt people. I don't want a lot of money. I just always dreamed, since I was a little girl, of finding that perfect prince just for me."

Mia and Brittany both nodded. They knew of those dreams too.

"All teenage girls dream of that," Mia told her.

"Am I destined to be alone?" Kimberly asked. "If I am, I may as well get started collecting my pet cats right now."

"No, of course not," Brittany told her. "The right guy will come along. He'll show up when you least expect it, and he'll whisk you off into that magic land of happy endings."

"Another damn love story," Kim moaned, and rested her head on the sofa pillow. "I hope so, because I don't even like cats."

Mia and Brittany laughed.

Mia rubbed Kim's back. "It's going to be okay, Kim. You'll see."

"What happened to sexy Mr. Elevator Man?" Brittany asked. "I thought you two hit it off in The Hamptons."

"Sterling?" Kim asked, lifting her head from the pillow. "I don't know. He scares me."

"Love is a scary thing," Mia told her. "You have to stick your heart out there, and risk getting it hurt in order to find your happy ending."

Kim lowered her head once again. A happy ending. Could Mr. Vespasian be Mr. Perfect Love Story? She had just met him, and they had shared one little kiss. That didn't mean that he was her destiny. Besides, she didn't even know what he did for a living. He worked for Vespasian, and probably as an executive in men's fashions. But... there were just too many variables. He was nice, and nice looking. He seemed like a gentleman. He was well groomed, nice job, great sense of humor. But the million dollar question was how did he feel about her? Was she jumping the gun here? Why was she even thinking about him right now? She should be thinking about her happily ever after man, not Sterling Williams. He certainly was not Mr. Happily Ever After. Was he?

Chapter Ten

Amaniko Somari was a fashion legend. Her name was a household name, one that reminded everyone of the glory years of fashion. She conjured images of Halston, Lagerfeld, Hermes, and Chanel. She had been a model for each of them, plus a number of other A-List designers. Discovered in Ethiopia in the Sixties, she had been airlifted out of a refugee camp with a large number of Falasha Jews. An orphan, she was taken to Israel, and adopted by a French Jewish family where she was relocated to Paris. It was on the streets of Paris where the thirteen year old with the copper colored skin, pale blue eyes, and long, silky, sandy colored hair was discovered. She was an exotic, among exotics. Her thin, lanky frame, awkward stand, and Mona Lisa smile, soon had her splashed across every fashion magazine in the world. And yes, she even made the cover of the French Vogue.

Amaniko modeled for more than thirty years, and along the way she amassed a fortune. First came her cosmetic line for women of color, then her very own modeling agency, and finally, her fashion house. Amaniko quickly became a fashion powerhouse, because rich White women loved her. Her designs reminded consumers of the age of Jackie Kennedy. Lime Green Hermes Kelly Bags, Louis Vuitton scarves tied around their heads, while sun bathing on the decks of a yacht. These were the looks that the Scarsdale crowd loved. Her designs were timeless, classic, elegant; they spoke of a gilded age, an age where America could do anything. An age where America could send a man to the moon, save an entire city from starvation by means of an airlift, and shake the conscious of an entire planet by way of a non violent civil rights movement. Amaniko's designs represented the best of America, and reminded people of all that was right with America. She and her clothing designs were both fashion icons.

Kimberly couldn't believe that Amaniko herself had agreed to meet with her. Of course it took a call from her father to one of his best friends, who in turn called a cousin, who was Amaniko's publicist. This fortunate meeting was taking place at

Ms. Emma's. The ambiance just seemed right.

"Thank you for meeting with me, Ms. Somari," Kim said, rising as the legendary designer approached the table. The two of them exchanged handshakes, and Amaniko seated herself.

"Sprite, with a lemon twist," Amaniko told the waiter.

"I'll have the same," Kim said, following the first rule in sales; Always have what the buyer or the boss is having. The waiter wrote down their orders, nodded, and quickly disappeared.

"Well, I'm going to be brutally honest with you, Ms. Neel," Amaniko said. "I have very little patience when it comes to designers. I personally have a hand in the design of everything with my company's name on it. We have a certain look, and we have to adhere rigidly to that look. Timeless elegance is what we strive for. Not trendy, not runway shock value, not to make the covers of Vogue, or Elle, or Ms., or any other magazine. We are part of the Town and Country set. My patrons are extremely wealthy, well bred, and predominantly White. They come from generations of wealth. They ride horses, play polo, hunt foxes, attend the Belmont races, the Kentucky Derby. Their children go to Groton, Philips Exeter, and Lawrence

Academies. Their children are legacies at Harvard, Yale, and Princeton. This is the Skull and Crossbones set. They vacation in St. Tropez, and St. Moritz. When the want to gamble, they don't go to Vegas, they go to Monte Carlos. Do you understand?"

Kimberly nodded. She was now more nervous than ever, and she felt wholly inadequate to the task. She gripped her design portfolio tight, and could feel beads of sweat forming at the top of her head.

"Good," Amaniko told her. "I won't waste your time, or mines. If your designs are inadequate, or don't mesh with my company's design philosophy, I'm going to tell you up front. However, with that said, there is nothing that I love more than to help a sister break into this industry and make a name for herself. If you have the talent, I will do all that I can to help you."

The waiter arrived with their drinks, placed them on the table, and again disappeared.

Amaniko held out her hand. "Well, let's see what you have."

With her hands shaking, Kimberly lifted her design portfolio to the table and opened it. Amaniko took a look at the first sketch, and sat her soda down. She waved for the waiter to come over.

"Well, you've past the first test," she told Kim. "Most designers don't get past the soda stage. Looks like we'll be having lunch together."

"Thank you!" Kimberly gushed. Her smile was now uncontrollable.

"I'll have the baked chicken," Amaniko told the waiter.

"I'll have the same," Kim said.

The waiter nodded, and retreated to the kitchen.

Amaniko flipped the first page in the design book, taking in the sketches on the second and third pages. "Promising. Very promising. Classy, elegant, timeless. The trick is to ask yourself, if you can visualize your customers wearing your designs fifty years from now, and still being in style. If the answer is yes, then you have designed something worthy of manufacture."

Kim couldn't believe that she was getting design advice from the legend herself. She felt as though her head was going to explode.

"Long, elegant, wool skirt and matching long sleeve jacket." Amaniko nodded. "I like. This is perhaps your best design thus far."

"Thank you."

Amaniko closed Kimberly's design portfolio

and peered across the table at her for several moments. "I'll tell you what. You take the designs that I spoke kindly of, and you design a collection around those, and I'll agree to meet with you and see what you have."

"Thank you so much!" Kim said, clasping Amaniko's forearm. "You can't imagine how much this means to me."

Amaniko nodded. "Yes, I can. But I don't mind. I see potential in you. Real potential."

*****

Trump Place was an event to be experienced, and not seen. It was not your run-of-the-mill luxury Manhattan apartment complex, by any stretch of the imagination. Personal service and attention to detail had been elevated to the level of decadence. From the around the clock concierge, to the fully equipped, state-of-the-art fitness center, to the club lounge with its creamy leather sofas, big screen TVs, and intricately carved billiard tables, to the complex's location itself. Right outside of the door, was Riverside Park, with all of its hiking, biking, and walking trails, along with its basketball, tennis, and handball courts. Two blocks down the street sat Lincoln Center, a boon to jazz, theater, ballet, opera, and symphony lovers. All of this luxury, service, and convenience did not come cheap, however, Trump Place was one of the most expensive places to live in the New York metropolitan area.

Kimberly climbed off of the elevator on the penthouse floor, huffing and puffing, and lugging her designs with her. She was late. Her meeting with Amaniko had went *very* well. The two of them enjoyed a late lunch, a stroll through Manhattan, and then a couple of lattes at Starbucks. Their conversation about fashion and about the history of modern American fashion had engrossed them. Time slipped by as the laughter and friendship grew through the afternoon and early evening. Before she knew it, her dinner date with Sterling was upon her.

Kimberly rang the doorbell; she was anxious, excited, exhilarated. Amaniko had her blood running. She hadn't been this excited about fashion in a long time. Finding someone with as much passion for design as she had was rare. Finding someone who knew a hundred times more about the industry than she did, was even rarer; especially someone who was willing to share their knowledge.

Sterling opened the door with a large smile on his face.

"I am *so* sorry!" Kim told him.

"No need for apologies," Sterling told her. "Hey, things happen." He stood to the side, and Kim entered. She peered around his three bedroom penthouse, taking in his ultra modern décor.

"Nice."

"Thank you."

"I didn't think this was your style," Kim said, smiling.

"What style is that?"

"This," Kim said, waving her hands around, and walking further into the room. "Swedish, Danish, Norwegian, Scandinavian, ultra modern, IKEA, whatever you call it, style."

Sterling threw his head back in laughter.

"What?" Kim asked, turning up her palms.

"What's wrong with my apartment?" Sterling asked.

"No, nothing," Kim said, shaking her head. "I love it. I just didn't picture this being you. You're looking more metro sexual everyday, Sterling."

"Ahhhh, so now I'm suspect."

"No, not suspect! Metro sexual is not gay."

"Metro sexual is code word for gay," Sterling

countered.

"It is not!" Kim told him. "It just means that you're a man of sophisticated and distinguished taste."

"Okay, so why can't a I just be a man of discerning taste?" Sterling asked. "Why do I have to be labeled metro sexual?"

"Oh, don't tell me you're phobic, Sterling?"

"I'm secure enough in myself to not worry about how others define me."

"Well, there you go." Kim said turning, and examining the apartment further. "Love that painting."

"Jacob Lawrence." Sterling told her. "It's an original. I have several of them here, as well as a few Paul Goodnights, and some Sharon Wilsons."

Kim lifted an eyebrow and spun in his direction. "I'm impressed. And surprised."

"Surprised? Why is that?"

"I figured that you would be more into collecting crazy white boys who cut off their ears."

Sterling laughed heartily. "I have a few of those as well."

"Ummmm hmmmmm," Kim said pursing her lips and nodding.

"Wait a minute," Sterling said, lifting his

palms. "You show up late, and you get me on the defensive. Is this a strategy you learned in high school?"

Kimberly laughed. "Okay, you caught me."

"Dinner is still hot."

"Is it?"

"I just finished cooking not too long ago. And I have the warming drawers turned up to their highest temperatures."

"So, what's for dinner?"

"Roasted and stuffed garlic Parmesean chicken breast, seared in a honey almond sauce, and served over a bed of rice pilaf."

"And you expect me to believe that *you* cooked that?" Kim asked.

"I did."

"Can you prove it?" Kim smiled.

"Prove it? I don't have to prove it!"

"After dinner, I'm searching your kitchen for signs of a caterer."

Sterling folded his arms and shifted his weight to one side. "What do you have there?"

Kim peered down at her portfolio. "This. Just some sketches."

Sterling held out his hand. "Let me see them. Are they yours?"

"No, I just carry other people's design sketches around with me. Of course they're mine, silly!"

Sterling opened the portfolio and flipped through the pages. "Wow, these are good."

"Really?"

"Yeah. These are really good." Sterling seated himself on his sofa, and Kim took the seat next to him. "Have you thought about going into the design side of the business?"

"That's my dream," Kim told him.

"Let me show some of your sketches to some people."

"At Vespasian?" Kim gasped. She immediately tried to close the portfolio. "No way!"

"Why not?"

"So that they can laugh at me? Oh no!"

"Laugh? Kim are you kidding me? These designs are really good."

Kimberly shook her head. "I'm not ready for Vespasian or anything like that."

"Kim, you have to believe in yourself, before others will believe in you," Sterling told her.

Slowly, Kim nodded and released the portfolio, allowing Sterling to continue to flip through it. He was right. She had to believe in herself, she thought. If she could sit down with

Amaniko, then she could face the corporate giants over at Vespasian. She just had to believe that she could; she had to believe that her designs were just as worthy as anyone else's. Sterling said that her designs were good, and he worked for Vespasian. Surely, he had seen thousands of designs and he knew what he was talking about.

Kim sat back an relaxed and went through her designs with Sterling. For some unknown reason she felt comfortable with him. For some unknown reason she felt a trust in this man that she had felt in no other.

Chapter Eleven

"It's the Yves St. Lauren, Oscar De La Renta, Mercedes Benz Charity Fashion Event, and I have to send two of you lucky bitches," Laquisha told them. "An entire weekend in New Orleans, taking in the sights, the sounds, the food, and hob knobbing with celebrities and supermodels. I wish that I could go myself, but I have to be in Paris that weekend for the Elle, Cover Girl, Peugeot fashion fair."

Jerome raised his hand timidly. "I'll go Paris."

"You are," she told him.

Jerome gasped and covered the mouth.

"I'm taking you along as my assistant," Laquisha told him. "I'm taking you, Mannie, and Lani with me. Aisha and Pam are going to Gstaad to cover the ski fashion show, and so that leaves Kimberly. Pezo will go with Kim to take the pictures, but that still leaves me without a writer to cover New Orleans. So, I guess this is your lucky day, Ms. Kimberly. You still think you're a writer?"

"Yes!" Kim said, excitedly.

"You'll have to write about the show in New Orleans, as well as generate ad revenue for the magazine. Can you handle both jobs?"

Kim nodded. "Yes."

"No bullshit, Kim!" Laquisha told her. "I want you to generate ad sales, and cover the fashion show. And put up a nightly blog on the internet about each day's events."

"I can do the blog," Pezo told her.

"Fine, do it," Laquisha ordered. "Kim, are you sure you're going to be able to handle this assignment?"

Again, Kimberly nodded. "I can do it."

Laquisha turned and peered out of her office window. "I can't believe I'm going to miss the de la Renta fashion event again this year! Man, do you have any idea what their executive gift bags have in them?"

Lani nodded. "I remember seeing one two years ago."

"Chanel No. 5 perfume, Louis Vuitton handbags, Hermes scarves, Escada sunglasses, Tiffany bracelets." Laquisha placed her hand over her forehead. "I'm talking Prada, Fendi, Juicy

Couture. Those gift bags are jam packed full of luxury shit. Plane tickets, vacation packages, hotel suites, spa gift certificates, luxury car rentals, all kinds of exotic soaps and candles, Godiva chocolates, imported wines and cheeses."

"All that in one basket?" Kim asked.

"Its called a gift *basket*, but its actually *baskets*," Laquisha explained.

"I get to get one of those?" Kim asked, trying to contain her smile.

"They are going to hook you up because you're there representing Mocha," Laquisha told her. "You need to bring my basket back to me."

"Girl, please!" Kim told her, hi-fiving Pamela.

"That's what I thought," Laquisha said, rolling her eyes. "That's why I ain't even try to go there. I know your scandalous ass would be all up in the shit anyway."

"Girl, save me some of that eucalyptus and cucumber shampoo that they give," Jerome told Kim.

"You got that," Kim said, hi-fiving him.

"Well, you all have your assignments," Laquisha told them. "I suggest that everyone wrap up what they're doing this week, and have your stuff packed by Thursday. Everyone is getting out of here on Thursday, and I'll see you all back in the office on Tuesday. I'll have my cell phone, and I'm taking my laptop, anyone need anything, I'm a phone call away. Let's get out there and get the story, and those dollars, and let's make next month our biggest and best issue yet."

*****

Wilson breezed into Sterling's office and tossed a newspaper onto the desk. "Seen this yet?"

Sterling lifted the newspaper and read from it. "Hugo Boss made clothes for the Nazi's during World War II. Old story. Why is anyone talking about that?"

"Not *that*!" Wilson told him. He flipped the newspaper. "This."

"Vespasian dominates fashion weekend in the Hamptons." Sterling read aloud.

"They said that Vespasian showed why it is the top fashion house in the industry," Wilson said gushing. "They called us *the top fashion house in the industry*!"

Sterling nodded his approval and smiled.

"All of the press coverage has been pretty much the same," Wilson continued. "They loved those damn leg wrap sandals, those T straps, the kimono, and pretty much our entire line up. I'm telling you, that girl, Gianna, she needs to be given full reign over an entire line of Vespasian products."

Sterling nodded. "Make it happen."

This time, is was Wilson's turn to nod. "Done. Also, while I'm here, I wanted to show you something."

"What is it?" Sterling leaned back in his overstuffed leather chair.

Wilson stood erect and snapped his fingers toward the door. Two workers entered the office holding open a large, black, silk comforter. In the center of the all black comforter was a massive golden V.

"What is it?" Sterling asked.

"Vespasian's new line of bedding." Wilson told him. "Luxurious, silk comforters, bed linens, and accessories."

Another set of workers walked in holding an all white silk comforter with Vespasian's logo embroidered in gold in the center of it.

"Nice," Sterling nodded. "I really like that one."

Another set of workers walked in with a gold comforter with Vespasian's logo embroidered in gold on the front of it.

"We're doing gold on gold, royal blue with gold logo, burgundy with gold logo, black with gold logo, black with black logo, white with gold logo, white with white logo, and for Christmas we're going to team up with Neiman Marcus and do a limited edition Vespasian platinum on platinum silk comforter and bedding set," Wilson explained.

A couple of workers began bringing in flatware and setting it on Sterling's desk. He lifted one of the plates and examined it. It was black, with a gold Vespasian logo in the center of it, and gold trim around the edges.

"Vespasian dishes?" Sterling asked, lifting an eyebrow.

Wilson smiled and nodded. "We're hot right now. We might as well go all out."

"Dishes?" Sterling asked again.

"Everyone has them," Wilson explained. "Versace has Rosenthal doing dishes for them. Vera Wang has dishes. All the top design houses have them. It's our turn."

Sterling lowered the plate to his desk and lifted another. This one was white with gold trim and gold logo.   Wilson lifted a wine glass that had been placed on Sterling's desk.

"We're going to do glassware, stemware, and flatware," Wilson told him. He handed Sterling the Vespasian wine glass.

"I love the designs," Sterling told him. "Don't get me wrong, I'm just wondering if we're ready for this."

"I don't understand. What do you mean, *if* we're ready for this?"

"I mean, between launching a full fledged women's line, are we moving too fast?" Sterling asked.

Wilson shook his head. "I don't think so. Sterling, relax. We're expanding, we're growing. Remember this forecast? We either grow, or we become irrelevant.   We had to get aggressive, remember? Well, our efforts are paying off. We're hot right now. Let's run with it."

Sterling nodded. "I'm inclined to agree. I just don't want to trip and fall. It took a lot of time and effort to build this company. Bankruptcy court is *not* where I want to end up."

"I got you," Wilson told him. "Oh, did I also tell you who else I got?"

Sterling sat up in his seat.

"I got Rhianna," Wilson told him. "She's going to runway for us in New Orleans."

"Get the heck out of here!" Sterling shouted.

"No, seriously," Wilson told him. "She's agreed to headline for us at the Mercedes Charity show."

"Wow," Sterling again leaned back in his chair. He was all smiles. "Good work."

"Of course."

Sterling lifted a gold serving tray with the Vespasian logo in the center of it, and held it up to the light. "This is gorgeous."

"Man, our flatware is going to kill the market," Wilson told him. "And wait until you see what I have coming in next week."

"What?"

"Dishes, with our Vespasian multi-color logo on them!" Wilson said excitedly. "Imagine that! Dishes, that match their handbags? They are going to go crazy!"

Sterling and Wilson broke into uncontrollable laughter.

"I'm glad that you work for me instead of the competition," Sterling told him.

"So when are you leaving?" Wilson asked.

"You mean, for New Orleans?" Sterling asked.

Wilson nodded.

"I'll fly out Friday morning, that way I can catch the opening events that evening."

"You're going to be okay flying in the same day?"

"Of course, why wouldn't I be?"

"Jet lag?"

"I'm not flying across an ocean," Sterling told him.

"Across a time zone though."

"I'll be okay. How's the executive search going?"

"Slow," Wilson exhaled. "Hard to find someone with the right vision. Good talent is rare these days."

"Oh, speaking of talent," Sterling said, snapping his fingers and sitting up. "Remember that woman I told you about. The one I asked out and everything."

"Kimberly?" Wilson asked, lifting an inquisitive eyebrow.

"That's the one," Sterling nodded. "She showed me some sketches the other night, and they were really good."

This time, Wilson lifted an eyebrow. "She's a designer?"

"She's an ad executive. But she wants to be a designer. She has some real talent."

Wilson nodded. "So, you want me to bring her in?"

"No, not yet. Maybe we can take a look at her sketches and see if they have some potential. If you feel the same way about them, then maybe we can bring her on board. But it's going to take some real convincing. The sister's got talent, but doesn't understand how much talent she's got."

Wilson nodded. "I'll look at them. Have her come by and bring them."

Sterling nodded. "I'll have her do it after I get back from New Orleans. I imagine she's going to New Orleans as well. Hmmm. I need to call her and see if she's going."

"Trying to hook up for a little bit of French Quarter romance?" Wilson asked.

Sterling shrugged. "Man, this sister is fierce. She is cooler than a fan, but that coolness turns to frozen tundra when it comes time to talk about her emotions. She ain't letting nobody crack that ice."

Chapter Twelve

"I'm walking out of the hotel right now," Kimberly told him. She flipped closed her cell phone as she ventured the last few steps out of the lobby and through the exit. Her mouth fell open when she saw the car that Sterling was waiting in.

It was a Bianco white, Ferrari F458 Italia Spyder. Spyder in Ferrari speak, means convertible. And Sterling had the top down so that everyone could see that rich, crème colored Italian leather interior.

Kimberly had seen Ferraris before. She saw them regularly on the streets of Manhattan, and certainly at celebrity fashion events across the country. But the fact that she was about to hop inside and take a spin in one, had her smiling uncontrollably.

"Now that's what I call a car," Kim told him.

Sterling waved his hand through the air

dismissing her statement. "It's just a rental."

"My company don't rent me cars like this," Kim smiled.

"Maybe you're with the wrong company."

"I am *definitely* with the wrong company!" Kim said, climbing inside. "So, what's on the agenda?"

"I arrived yesterday afternoon, and spent all night schmoozing, drinking, and partying with industry big wigs," Sterling told her. "Before I go through another night of that, I need a break to clear my head."

"Really?"

"Yeah," Sterling nodded. "And I know the perfect place for us to get lost for the entire day."

"All day?" Kim asked, lifting an eyebrow. "You know, some of us have work to do."

"And you'll do it. You know that things don't start jumping until night time. We'll be back by then."

"Okay, whatever you say," Kim said, throwing her hands up.

"You're going to love it," Sterling told her. "Besides, you can't come to Louisiana, without seeing the *real* Louisiana."

"The real Louisiana?" Kim asked nervously.

It didn't sound right.

"There's more to southern Louisiana than the French Quarter," Sterling said with a smile. "Most people would be surprised to learn that."

Kim shrugged. "Okay, you've piqued my curiosity, Mr. Sterling. I'm all yours for the day. Show me the real Louisiana."

Sterling shifted the car into gear and slowly pulled off. "You might want to put on your seat belt. Highway 61, here we come!"

*****

Located in West Feliciana Parish, Greenwood Plantation was the ultimate manifestation of the power, wealth, and class that had been amassed along the banks of the Mississippi. It had been erected in 1835 by Ruffin Barrow, a member of one of the wealthiest families in the Mississippi valley during those times. The Barrow's owned not only enormous cotton and sugar plantations on both sides of the river, but thousands of slaves as well. As beautiful and elegant as those mansions were, their history was tarnished with the shame of the ultimate sin.

Greenwood was typical of the veranda houses of the nineteenth century South. Typical, in all but its size, that is. The mansion boasted thirty-five foot long Doric columns that wrapped around the entire perimeter of the house. So grand was Greenwood's scale, that the rooftop of a car wouldn't reach the top of the porch balustrades. Greenwood was truly a sight to behold.

"This place is so beautiful!" Kimberly declared, walking through the rear gardens, and clutching Sterling's arm. "I feel like Scarlett O'Hara in *Gone With The Wind*. I do declare!"

Sterling laughed at her exaggerated Southern accent. "I can't come to Louisiana without visiting the plantations here. Especially the ones along the Mississippi."

"Oh really? And why is that? Are you originally from Louisiana?"

"No," Sterling said, shaking his head. "I was raised in Savannah, and later Charleston."

"Ahhh," Kimberly nodded. "That explains your love of old Southern architecture."

"A little bit," Sterling conceded. "But in all actuality, I don't think a person could be an artist, and not love the architecture. It's so romantic, so powerful, so historic. It speaks to a bygone era of gentility. Mint juleps, hoop skirts, gentlemanly conduct; I love that era."

Kimberly laughed. "You love that era? Have you forgotten that our people were slaves during those genteel times?"

"Of course not," Sterling said, shaking his head. "Come on, let's go over here. I want to show you where the slave quarters used to be."

"I'll bet you there was nothing elegant about those cabins," Kim said softly.

Sterling led Kimberly across the plantation grounds to an area marked by nothing more than a simple plaque.

"This is hollowed ground," Sterling said softly.

Kimberly nodded.

"This is where it all happened. This is where the foundation of Black love was laid."

"What?" Kim craned her neck toward him. "What do you mean? Are you saying that Black people didn't know love until they were brought over here in chains?"

"No, of course that's not what I'm saying!" Sterling told her. "But you have to distinguish between the two. The love that our ancestors knew on the African continent, was African love. It was something that was grounded in history, and tradition, and sanctioned by the spirits, the ancestors, the village, the entire world. It was good love, legal love; *sanctioned* love. But the love that our ancestors created over here, was a completely different animal."

Sterling knelt down and pulled a wild flower from the ground. He closed his eyes, held the flower to his nose for several moments and inhaled deeply.

"We created an entirely new culture for ourselves over here," he continued. "Many tribes, many cultures, different languages, all came together to create a new *Black American* culture. And out of that culture, out of the pith and mire and miasmic conditions of slavery, came a new kind of love. A love that few other cultures have known. A true love."

Kimberly swallowed hard. She was falling in love with this man, with each word that he spoke.

Sterling pointed toward the ground where the slave cabins would have been. "At night, she held his head in her arms, and whispered away the nightmares of the day. She rubbed healing roots on his torn, ripped, open back. She took him into her, with the promise of a better tomorrow."

Tears fell from Kimberly's eyes. "I never thought about it like that."

"Most people haven't," Sterling said softly. "They think plantation, and slavery, but they never think about the lives of the actual people. Our ancestors were alive, they were people with feelings, emotions, hopes, and dreams. They didn't just pick cotton twenty four hours a day. At night, in these cabins, they survived, they dreamed, they loved, and they built lives together."

"Most people are of the opinion that slavery destroyed the black family," Kim said, wiping away her tears.

Sterling shook his head. "That's a misconception. How could it have destroyed the Black family, when they loved one another in a way that few of us could even begin to fathom in this day and age. Do you realize that that Black man knelt down by his woman's side at night, held her, caressed her, and built her back up after Master had had his way with her? Can you even begin to fathom the kind of love that he had for her? To take her and love her, when night after night she staggers back into the cabin bleeding, brutalized, with tattered garments hanging from her body. Can you imagine that kind of commitment? Can you imagine the love that he had inside of him to raise not just his children, but her and Master's children as well? And to love them all equally, as his own? That's more than just being there for somebody, more than just seeing one another through a storm. That was a love that was ordained by God Himself. *My God*, the history behind these plantations! Yes, I love the architecture, but that's because the architecture is part of the story, the history; it speaks to the times. It was in this era when grace and beauty and charm reigned throughout the land. It was in this era when a people's love and faith and hope sustained an entire race."

Kimberly peered into Sterling's eyes and realized that she had found a man with a depth and sophistication and intelligence that was unfathomable. John was doctor, and he could do wonderful things. He could save lives, mend wounds, heal the sick. He was educated, but it was an education that was technical. Sterling was educated, but it was an education with depth. He truly understood his place in the world, he understood the history of his country, and the history of his people. Here was a man who could speak about love, and truly understand the meaning of it.

What was love? What did it mean? How did it manifest itself? He could answer those questions, and because he could answer those questions, she knew that he could love her.

Kimberly leaned forward and kissed Sterling. Their lips met; timidly at first. The first peck, the second, a gentle third. Then finally, their lips locked with a full embrace. It was as if their bodies were saying hello to one another for the first time.

Kim felt herself floating. She was lost in time and space, and for the first time, was in no hurry to return to reality. Sterling could love. And so could she. She knew that she could love, although at one time she had vowed that she would never love another. And then, when loneliness set in, she swore that she would never be able to *find* another. All of the men that she had been introduced to since she and John's relationship ended, had been losers. Guys with great looks, great jobs, and severe social or mental flaws. Most of them had been frightened of commitment; momma's boys. Others were want-to-be-players, some were kids in grown up bodies, and some were just plain assholes. And now, she was locked in an embrace with a guy unlike any she had ever met.

She could love again. In fact, there was no

need for her mind to pretend to be debating the issue. That she was now in love with Sterling, was a foregone conclusion. How this would play into her life, she did not know. The last thing she wanted, or needed, were complications. But then again, the very last thing she wanted, was to walk through life alone.

"Wow, what was that about?" Sterling asked, after their lips parted.

Kimberly peered into his eyes. "I'm falling in love with you, Sterling."

It had taken him by surprise. But it was a pleasant surprise. "Fall right in."

"Is that going to scare you away?" Kim asked with a smile.

"Nothing and no one, could drive me away from you," Sterling said softly.

Again, their lips met.

Chapter Thirteen

Sterling opened the small door and helped Kimberly into the rear seat of the horse drawn carriage. The night was mild, and the sky clear, revealing a heaven that was teeming with stars. It was the perfect night for lovers.

"I can't believe you!" Kimberly said, still exhilarated by the night's events. The charity fashion show had been unlike any event she had ever attended. It was an event that catered to the big wigs of the industry, and small fish like her rarely got a chance to bask in the greatness of the industry's inner circle. And the only reason she had been able to do so tonight, had been because she was arm in arm with Sterling. "How do you know those people?"

Sterling shrugged. "They're friends."

"Friends, Sterling?" Kimberly asked, still in shock. "I have friends! Those people are *not* friends, they're legends!"

Sterling threw his head back in laughter.

"Where too, sir?" the driver asked.

"Show us the beauty of Old New Orleans," Sterling told him.

"Yes, sir," the driver said, pulling off.

"Sterling, how in the heck do you know Donatella Versace?" Kimberly asked. "Or Giorgio Armani? Or Marc Jacobs? Or Gianfranco Ferre?"

"Old friends," Sterling told her. "I've known Marc for years. Gianfranco also."

"That was Yves Saint Laurent that you were talking to by the ice sculpture!" Kimberly gushed. She had been like a kid in a candy store. Or more like a kid at a super hero convention. "I can't believe I got to meet Lagerfeld, Gaultier, Oscar de la Renta, Christian Lacroix, and Roberto Cavalli!"

Kimberly bounced up and down in the carriage seat. "I can't believe Caroline Herrera called you her boyfriend!"

"I've known Caroline for a long time," Sterling told her. "She's like an aunt to me. She helped me so much when I first started in the business."

"How do you know all those people?" Kimberly shouted. "What do you do at Vespasian?

How is it that Ralph Lauren knows you by name? How is it that *Tom Ford* of all people, comes up to you and puts you in a head lock, and play wrestles with you at one of the biggest fashion events in the country? Who are you?"

Sterling laughed. "Calm down. Tom is an old friend. I've known him since his days at Gucci."

"Why were they asking you about Vespasian's fall collection?"

Sterling shrugged. "They were just joking. Everybody wants to know what everyone else is planning for the fall. But in the bigger scheme, no one really cares what the other guy is doing. Not on this level. Well, they care, but it doesn't matter. Tom is going to put out what Tom is going to put out. Miuccia is going to put out what she is going to put out, and Marc is going to do Marc. So in the end, it really doesn't matter."

"Miuccia?" Kimberly asked, lifting an inquisitive eyebrow.

"Yeah." Sterling said, matter of fact. And then he caught on. "Oh, Miuccia. I'm sorry. Miuccia Prada."

"Prada?"

"Yeah, Prada."

Kimberly's mouth fell slightly open. "You

know her?"

"Yeah," Sterling laughed. "You do to. She was standing next to me and talking to us half the evening."

Kimberly gasped. "*That woman*! The one in the black dress! That was her?"

Sterling nodded and laughed.

Kimberly felt like fainting. She had been talking fashion with a fashion giant. She felt embarrassed. "You could have *told* me who she was!"

"I thought you knew."

"Sterling, I'm an ad executive at a fashion magazine," Kimberly explained. "I sell ads to corporate bean counters. I *never* get to meet the type of people who I met tonight. *Never.* I'm not on a first name basis with anyone like that, and to be honest with you, I've never really met anyone who was."

"I introduced you to them."

Kimberly exhaled and peered out of the carriage. "I don't know you, Sterling. You scare me."

"Why?"

"One minute, I think that I have you pegged, and then you just explode my perceptions of you.

148

You kill my comfort with you, and make me realize that I really don't know you. That scares me."

"What scares you?"

"Not knowing who you really are!"

"I'm me! I'm Sterling Williams. I haven't hidden anything from you, or tried to deceive you, or been dishonest with you in any way!"

"Those people," Kimberly continued. "Those ones you so nonchalantly call your friends. Who has friends like *that*, Sterling?"

"I work at one of the largest, most prestigious fashion houses in the industry. You don't think that I would know the leading designers in the industry? Come on, this is the industry that I'm in. Those people are my peers, and some of my fiercest competitors. We've worked together for various charity events, and competed on runways all over the planet. We see each other dozens of times a year. You don't think that we would talk to one another and eventually develop a friendship?"

Kimberly thought about it, and grudgingly nodded. He was right. This was the industry that he was in. He was an executive at a major design house. He would know many of the world's top designers. What was wrong with her? Why was she acting the way she was acting? Was she subconsciously trying to drive him away? Was she trying to ruin things before they got started?

"Why are you trying to put me inside a neat little box, Kim?" Sterling asked softly. "I've never tried to put you in one. Yesterday, we talked about Black love, and what it meant to us. Well, one other thing that it means to me, is giving the person you love, the freedom to be their self. Love is unconditional acceptance of the person as they are, and not as you want them to be. Love me as Sterling, and all that I am. And I will love you as Kimberly, and all that that entails."

"Driver, take us to the Marriott," Kim said.

"The Marriot?" Sterling asked.

Kimberly nodded. "I want to go to my hotel."

"Are you okay?" Sterling asked.

Kimberly nodded. "I'm perfect, Sterling."

*****

Kimberly pulled Sterling into her motel room, and kissed him with the ferocity of a wild lioness. She wanted to devour every inch of him. He was a kind, sensitive, intelligent, educated, super sexy man. He had taste, and style, and he wasn't some under cover brother. He stayed well groomed and well manicured, and yet he never obsessed over his looks. He was a well grounded, Christian man, with a belief in God, and a knowledge of history. He was everything that she had dreamed about having in a man, and then some.

"Are you sure you want to do this, Kim?" Sterling asked.

She nodded. "Are you ready?"

"I'm ready," he told her. "The questions is, are you. I don't share my body with just anyone. If we do this, then this means that we are in a monogamous relationship. Are you ready for that kind of commitment? Are you ready to commit to a serious relationship?"

Kimberly pulled him close and kissed him again, giving him his answer.

Sterling ran his hand over her blouse, unbuttoning it slowly. He lifted her into the air, and carefully carried her to the bed. Kimberly laid back on the bed, not knowing if she was truly ready to give herself to this man. Sterling parted her shirt, and kissed her stomach with tiny pecks, working his way around her navel and up the center of her torso.

"Here, unfasten this," Kimberly said,

breathing heavily. She arched her back, giving him room to slide his hand beneath her, and undo the clasp on her bra. Sterling deftly performed the maneuver with one hand, freeing her breast for his consumption. Which he did immediately.

Sterling took her right nipple into his mouth and sucked gently. The warmth of his mouth and gentle suction made her ready to explode. It had been a while since a man had done this to her.

"Oh, Sterling!"

Sterling's tongue made its way to her other breast, where he engulfed it. Again, she felt herself ready to explode. Sterling worked his way down her body to her navel where he paused, and deftly unfastened the clasp on her skirt. Kimberly slid her skirt, hosiery, and underwear down, and then kicked it off onto the floor. She climbed further back onto the bed, and laid back once again.

Sterling kissed Kim around her belly button, and then moved further south. Kim opened her legs, and Sterling parted her paradise with his tongue. It surprised her.

"Oh, Sterling!" Kimberly moaned, arching her back, and gripping his head.

Sterling worked his tongue. His strokes were deep, lashing strokes. He licked slowly at first, building in pace with each of her passionate moans. Kim found that she couldn't control herself. She clasped his head and gyrated her waist, while moaning uncontrollably.

"Sterling!"

Sterling took her labia into his mouth and sucked and licked alternately. The suction pressure on her labia caused her to orgasm fiercely. Kimberly arched her back and cried out passionately. It felt as though she had a river flowing inside of her.

"Sterling, I'm about to..."

Sterling placed his mouth over her vagina, and sucked with the intensity of a Hoover vacuum. His suction caused her to immediately orgasm a second time. The streaming juices inside of her raced through her vagina and into Sterling mouth. She could feel her cum being sucked out of her, and it caused her to let out a passionate cry.

"*Oh.... Sterling! Oh, God! Sterling! Oh, help...me...*"

Sterling unbuttoned his shirt and tossed it to the floor. Then off came his t shirt, and then his shoes, socks, and trousers. Kimberly kissed him all over his chest, pulling off his underwear, and then pulling him onto her. She wanted him inside of her badly. She *needed* him inside of her.

"Come on," she said softly, almost pleading.

They kissed passionately once again. Her tongue gliding over his neck. His mouth engulfing her ear lobe. They fumbled with one another clumsily in their hurried passion. Kimberly lifted her right leg, and then guided Sterling into her.

"Oh!" she cried out, as he plunged into her deeply. "Sterling!"

"Oh, Kim!" he grunted.

Sterling began to gyrate slowly, while beneath him Kimberly found her rhythm counter-clockwise. She didn't know whether it was because she hadn't been with a man in a long time, or whether it was because he was well endowed, but she quickly found herself reaching another climax. Her nails dug into Sterling's muscular back as she came like there was no tomorrow.

"Sterling!" she cried out. "What are you doing to me?"

Sterling was concentrating on other things. He was busy kissing her neck and face, and twisting, grinding, and digging deep inside of her.

"Sterling," she tried to speak, but found her mouth being muffled by kisses. He was stroking hard, and the fact that she couldn't get a word in edge wise, really turned her on. He was handling his business in a way that none before him had. He had her open in a hotel bed, punishing her deeply, and all she could do was hold him tightly and moan.

"Sterling!" she cried out, cumming once again.

What had she gotten herself into, she wondered? She hadn't been sexed like this before. He was deep inside of her stomach, and he wasn't showing any signs of letting up anytime soon. She had heard of experiences like this. Even dreamed of it. Being punished by a King Kong dong all night long, and being damn near helpless to stop it. The only thing she could do was go along for the ride. She just hoped that she would be able to walk in the morning. It would be embarrassing to try to climb out of bed and fall flat on her face.

"Sterling," Kimberly moaned and breathed in heavily. He didn't answer, as he was too busy sticking and jabbing. Kimberly adjusted beneath him and got comfortable. She knew that she was in for a long night. He had been at it for more than forty five minutes already, and he hadn't even broken a sweat.

Just Another Damn Love Story

Chapter Fourteen

Mia pulled her panties from between her buttocks and seated herself between Brittany's legs. Brittany rubbed conditioner on Mia's hair, and then commenced to brushing. Kimberly turned away from the wall of windows toward them.

"I don't know what else to say," Kimberly said, exhaling.

"Girl, tell us again about how *hung* Mr. Sterling was?" Brittany said laughing.

"See, that's what I'm talking about!" Kimberly told them.

"What?" Brittany asked, turning her palms up.

"What are you talking about?" Mia asked, exchanging glances with Brittany.

"You two only hear what you want to hear!" Kim protested.

"What?" Mia asked, smiling.

"I poured my heart out to you, and the only

thing you heard was how big he was, and how he screwed my brains out until the sun came up!"

"Ummmm," Brittany moaned, and placed the corner of a pillow between her teeth and bit down.

"See!" Kim said protesting. "You nasty bitches only care about the freaky shit!"

Mia and Brittany exchanged glances and laughed heartily.

"Kim, you're making a mountain out of a mole hill," Mia told her.

"Yeah, he doesn't seem like a bad guy," Brittany added.

"I just don't know," Kimberly whined. "Guys, I'm here because I need your help. Give me some advice. Some of that good sisterly advice that you always manage to give."

"Kim, you don't need our advice," Brittany told her. "Since when do you need someone else to tell you how *your* heart feels?"

Kimberly exhaled, shook her head, and peered out of the window once more. "I just don't know about him. There's something that's just not right, something that I can't put my finger on."

"But you slept with him *anyway*?" Mia asked, lifting an eyebrow.

"Yeah, but..." Kim stuttered, trying to find the

right words. "Sometimes, he makes you feel as if you are the only two people on the planet. He's warm and sincere, kind, thoughtful, full of this beautiful insight. But..."

"But what?" Brittany asked. "But he knows a lot of celebrities, so what!"

"Yeah, like when's that ever been a *bad* thing?" Mia added.

"No, you two don't understand!" Kimberly told them. "He was play wrestling with *Tom Ford*, like they were *brothers* or something. It was crazy!"

"Okay?" Mia said, turning her palms up.

"Okay? Okay!" Kim began pacing frantically. "This is Tom Ford we're talking about! Mr. Gucci himself! And then he's talking to Ralph Lauren, Marc Jacobs, Miuccia Prada like they were just family members or something."

Kim lifted Brittany's electric blue, leather, Marc Jacobs bag off of the sofa and then grabbed Mia's black Prada bag off of the table, and held them both up in the air. "*Hello*, Marc Jacobs, Miuccia Prada! We have their *handbags*! And this man knows them *personally*? C'mon, guys, isn't that just a little freaky to you? Doesn't that spook you just a *little*?"

"*Hell no!*" Mia said. "*Girl*, I'd be trying to

get the hook up!"

Brittany and Mia hi-fived, and then Brittany placed her hand to the side of her face like she was talking on a cell phone. "Yo, Miuccia! Girl, when's your next bag coming out, and can you send me one before it hits the stores. You know how we do it!"

"Right!" Mia said, again hi-fiving Brittany.

"Kim you are going crazy, over something that you don't need to go crazy about," Brittany told her. "He's a good man. Well educated, helluva job, handsome, treats you like a princess…"

"And can go all night!" Mia added. "Bitch you're tripping!"

Kimberly placed her hands over her face and then rubbed her eyes. "You two don't get it, and there's no way to explain it to you."

"Kim, do you like him?" Brittany asked.

Kimberly peered out of the window toward the Hudson. The sun was reflecting off of the water, giving it a brilliant, red-orange glow. It was beautiful. She thought about Brittany's question. She thought that she knew that answer to it; in fact, she thought that she had figured that one out a long time ago.

Sterling was a good man. He understood love, and yes, he understood her. She felt safe with him, even if not entirely comfortable. He wasn't dangerous, just hard to figure out. What was it about him that made people want to flock toward him? What made people want to befriend him? What made people just want to be in his presence? She too loved being around him. He made her smile, just being near. Whether it was the way he winked at her across the room, or that smile he gave her that made her feel desired. What was it about him?

How could a man be so open, so honest, and yet so mysterious? She had been to his apartment. Tonight, she was going to his home. She had been to Vespasian, his place of employment. She had all of his telephone numbers, from his Blackberry and iPhone, to his home number, to his office number. He wasn't hiding anything, and yet...

"Girl, does he treat you good?" Mia asked.

"Yes," Kimberly said, snapping out of her thoughts. "He does, he treats me really well. And yes, I do like him, I like him a lot."

Could she tell them? Of course she could, they were her best friends, her sisters in fact.

"I told him that I loved him," Kimberly said softly.

"What?" Mia leaped off of the carpet.

161

"You told him that?" Brittany asked.

Kimberly nodded.

"It was during sex right?" Mia asked. "If it was while he was putting the smack down on your candy ass then it doesn't count, right?"

"Right!" Brittany agreed. "You can say anything during really great sex and get a pass for it the next day."

Kimberly laughed. "I don't get a pass. I don't want a pass."

"Kim!" Mia shouted. "How could you? I know I taught you better than this!"

"You can't tell the first sausage you get in years that you love it!" Brittany told her.

"You want to scare the poor guy off?" Mia asked. "You're just getting started!"

"Men can't handle the *L* word until after you've been dating for at least a couple of years," Brittany explained.

"They're like animals," Mia told her. "Think of them like wild lions, and you're like Siegfried, or Roy. You have to build up their trust."

"Yeah, you have to talk gently to them, pet them, feed them for a couple of years," Brittany added. "And then you can move into their cages with them."

"And after they're comfortable with you being around, then you can use the L word in front of them," Mia explained.

Kim placed her hands on her hips. "Guys, it's that kind of thinking that gets us into trouble in the first place. Besides, he…"

"He what?" Brittany asked. "He said it first?"

"No," Kim said, shaking her head.

"He said it back?" Mia asked.

"Not exactly," Kim told them.

"You said 'I love you', and he didn't say 'I love you' back?" Brittany asked.

Kim shook her head. "I told him that I was falling in love with him, and he told me to fall right in."

"Ugggghhhh!" Mia pulled at the ponytails that Brittany had just placed in her hair. *"I can't believe you*, Kim!"

"Are you really falling in love with this guy?" Brittany asked.

Kimberly stared at them for several seconds, before slowing nodded.

"That must have been some really good…" Mia started, before Brittany elbowed her. "What?"

"Okay, then, *Houston we have a problem*," Brittany declared.

Mia exhaled. "If you're really falling for this guy, then I guess it's time we give him a thorough examination."

"And investigation," Brittany added. "It's time we called out the circle and find out every little detail about Mr. Sterling Williams."

"Thanks, guys," Kim told them.

"Hey, if he's going to have our sister's heart in his hands, then we're going to make damn sure that he doesn't break it," Mia told her.

The three of them gathered in a circle and hugged.

"Hey, you're meeting him tonight for dinner right?" Mia asked.

Kim nodded. "Yeah."

"Get a piece of his hair," Mia told her. "I'll have my friend over in the CSI lab run it through his database and do a fifty state check on Mr. Sterling. If he's gotten so much as a parking ticket in Alaska, we'll know about it."

"Mia!" Kim and Brittany both cried out in unison.

Mia shrugged. "Just trying to help."

*****

The Estates of Valhalla was the premiere community in northern New Jersey. Located in Montville, New Jersey within the upscale Morris County, Valhalla was a luxurious community of old world estates, nestled on four acre lots. Located only twenty eight miles from midtown Manhattan, the Estates of Valhalla were home to some of New York's biggest movers and shakers. The cheapest mansion within the estates priced out at over three million dollars. Sterling's mansion, was one of the largest in the community.

Kimberly pulled up to Sterling's palatial French country style estate, and found herself nearly breathless. Not only did the massive mansion take her breath away, but the Rolls Royce Cornice, the Bentley Continental GT, The Bugatti Veyron, and the Lamborghini Aventador sitting in the driveway, left her speechless. It all made her very nervous again. Who was this man who lived in this massive mansion, had an apartment in Trump Place, drove Rolls Royces, Ferrari, and Lamborghini, and moved in the same circles as Oscar de la Renta, Caroline Herrera, and Jean-Paul Gaultier? *Who was he?* The question that really scared her, was why was he interested in her? Was he simply toying with *her*? What could she offer him?

"Hey!" Sterling said, opening the front door to his mansion.

"What?" Kim asked, lifting an eyebrow. "No housekeeper?"

Sterling laughed. "Actually, I have three. But they've been given the night off."

She was being sarcastic, but it backfired. He had three.

Sterling waved for her to enter. Kimberly stepped inside, and could do nothing but gasp.

The home was decorated in French Empire. The interior furnishings, moldings, and gilded walls and ceilings looked as if she had just stepped inside of the French royal palace at Versailles. All of the Louis's were represented in the furnishings. Chairs from Louis XIV, settees from Louis XV, armoire, mirrors, tables, etc. from those Louis and others.

A dual staircase with intricate wrought iron banisters greeted visitors upon entrance into the foyer. A massive stain glass dome sitting some forty five feet up topped the foyer, while luxurious imported marble floors ran throughout. Kim peered into the grand dining hall just off of the foyer. Gold ceiling tiles, and a massive Swarovski crystal chandelier made her clasp her chest. Her heart felt as though it had skipped a beat.

"Sterling, this house!" Kim gushed.

"What?"

Kim shook her head in befuddlement. "I can't believe this house!"

"Okay, you teased me about my apartment being too modern," Sterling told her. "So now, you're going to say that my house is too what?"

"I'm not going to say *anything* bad about this house," Kim told him. I can't believe it." She started down a central hall, and came to a gallery hall that led to the formal living room.

"Is this what I think it is?" Kim asked.

Sterling nodded. "A Picasso? Yeah."

Kim's mouth fell slightly open.

"Oh, that's right. I forgot, you *like* the White boys," Sterling laughed. "I told you that I kept them here at my home. Well, here they are. Picasso is there, there, and there. Monet is over there. Renoire is over there and there. Rembrant is over there. Dago is over there and there. Cezanne is all over the house. I also have two more Rembrants, three more Monets, two more Picassos, and three more Renoires. Since you *like* the White boys."

Kimberly laughed and punched him. "Stop

it!"

"Me, I'll take my Jacob Lawrences and Paul Goodnights over the White boys anytime."

"How did you manage to build up this kind of private collection?" Kim asked.

"Just catching them whenever they go up for sale," he told her.

"I know Vespasian doesn't pay you this kind of money!" Kim said, shaking her head.

Sterling looked at her and smiled.

Kim lifted her hand. "Sorry, I'm not trying to get into your personal business. But *damn*!"

Sterling nodded toward the rear of the house. "C'mon, I'll show the rest of the house, and then we can come back downstairs and eat. I have the lobsters on the grill outside."

"Lobster?" Kim asked, lifting an eyebrow.

"Lobsters, shrimp marinade in a delectable honey, garlic, and butter sauce. Stuffed crab rolls, grilled salmon, a fresh Cesar salad, asparagus tips with a lemon garlic sauce that will make you cry. And a nice chilled bottle of Krug waiting for us out near the Jacuzzi. And if you feel up to it, I had some fresh strawberries dipped in white chocolate."

Kimberly closed her eyes and swayed slightly. She knew that after tonight, she was going to have trouble walking again.

Chapter Fifteen

Purchase Estates in Westchester County was one of the areas most prestigious developments. It was home to many of Westchester County's most prominent residents, and homes within the community started at two million dollars. At least back when one could actually buy a home within the community. Long since sold out, the asking prices now started at four million dollars. Dr. Neel bought his Tudor style mansion at the pre-construction bargain price of 1.6 million dollars, back when the community first opened up for development. He often touted the purchase in Purchase, as one of his best investment decisions ever. It was in this investment where Kimberly and her sister Beverly grew up.

"Pass me the celery," Marjorie told her daughter.

Mother and daughter were inside of the home's

171

quarter of a million dollar kitchen. Custom cabinetry, granite counter tops, and custom, stainless steel, Sub Zero and Wolff appliances dominated the room. The kitchen had even been featured on the Sub Zero-Wolff website at one time. It was Marjorie Neel's pride and joy, as well as her favorite part of the home.

"Celery!" Marjorie repeated.

Kim handed her mother the celery, and then continued to chop her onions.

"So what brought you up to Westchester today?" Marjorie asked.

"I came to see you and Daddy," Kim said.

"And what a wonderful surprise it was to see you," Thornton said, winking at her from the family room. He unfolded his newspaper and leaned back in his easy chair.

Marjorie glared over the bar into the family room, where her husband was seated. "Don't encourage her, Thornton. You know as well as I do, that she has never come home on her own accord."

"Mother!" Kimberly protested.

"And she walked in, washed her hands, and began helping prepare dinner?" Marjorie glared at Kim. "The only question left, is how much?"

"How much?" Kim huffed. "Mom, I don't

need any money."

"Sure you do. You're thin as a rail. That job of yours doesn't pay diddley squat. And you just came back from New Orleans."

"I'm not rail thin, my job takes care of my bills, and the trip to New Orleans was work, so it was paid for by my job."

"How was your trip, dear?" Thornton asked from the family room.

"It was wonderful!" Kim gushed. "I got to meet some of my favorite designers!"

"Any of them offer you a job?" Marjorie asked.

"I have a job, Mother."

"A *real* job? Like in their accounting department?" Marjorie persisted.

"Who did you get to meet, Sweetheart?" Thornton asked.

"I got to meet Marc Jacobs, Caroline Herrera, Oscar de le Renta, Christian Lacroix, Karl Lagerfeld, Roberto Cavalli, Jean-Paul Gaultier, Ralph Lauren, Tom Ford, and Muiccia Prada, just to name a few."

"Wow, that's fantastic, Sweetheart!" Thornton told her. "Did you get any autographs?"

"Dad!"

"What?"

"I couldn't ask for their autographs!"

"Why not?"

"Because, that would have made me look... unprofessional."

"Admiring someone's work so much that you want their autograph makes you look unprofessional?" Thornton asked. "I would think that it makes you look like a student of the industry; someone who appreciates talent, and skill, and art."

"Oh, *hush*, Thornton!" Marjorie told him. "You are so old fashioned. The girl can't go around begging people for their autographs."

"What is it about this day and age, when you can't appreciate another person's work?" Thornton grumbled. "You can't say job well done anymore, or people accuse you of being a sycophant. That's what's wrong with young people today. They have no sense of direction or purpose, because they refuse to accept guidance. They don't believe in mentors anymore."

Marjorie huffed. "So you actually got a chance to meet Oscar de la Renta, and Caroline Herrera?"

Kimberly paused, and then smiled. Those were two of her mother's favorite designers. Coco

Chanel, being the third. "Yes."

"What was she like?" Marjorie asked grudgingly.

"She was wonderful," Kim said. "Very elegant, very gracious, very warm."

Marjorie would never admit that her daughter's job was interesting, but still. Meeting Oscar de la Renta, Tom Ford, Marc Jacobs, and Caroline Herrera had impressed her. "So, how did you manage to meet them? Did they have you picking up the chairs after the fashion show?"

"Ha, ha, real funny, Mother."

"Give the child a break, Marjorie," Thornton called out from his easy chair.

"Oh, *read your newspaper*, Thornton!" Marjorie shouted back.

"I got to meet them through a mutual acquaintance," Kimberly said. Almost instantly, she regretted it.

"A mutual acquaintance?" Marjorie asked, lifting an eyebrow. Her motherly instincts were buzzing full time. She smelled the codeword for boyfriend.

"Yeah," Kimberly shrugged. She raked the onions she had chopped into a Tupperware bowl, and then pulled some seasoning from the cabinet.

"Here, I'll take that," Marjorie told her, removing the pan of cornbread from in front of her daughter. "I'll make the dressing." She didn't want anything to distract Kimberly from her barrage of questions.

"Here, I can do it," Kimberly told her. "You finish up the turkey and the candied yams. I can handle the cornbread dressing."

"The turkey is fine," Marjorie said overly polite. "There's really nothing left for you to do. Sit down and take a load off, darling."

Kimberly's suspicions were now confirmed. Her mother was about to drill into her like Exxon Mobile into a new oil find. Kimberly nervously edged her bottom onto the bar stool next to the kitchen island, and then peered around for something to do.

"Did your acquaintance fly down to New Orleans with you?" Marjorie asked.

"With me?" Kimberly shook her head. "No."

"Hmmmph." Marjorie began mixing her cornbread. "Well, is your friend in the fashion industry as well?"

"Yeah."

Thornton burst into laughter. He knew what his wife was doing, as well as what his daughter was

176

doing. He knew that Kimberly's one word answers were driving his wife crazy.

"Well, what does your friend do?" Marjorie asked.

Kimberly shrugged. "I don't know."

"You don't know?" Marjorie asked lifting an eyebrow.

"Not exactly."

"Not exactly? Must not really be a that much of a friend. How is Brittany and Mia?"

"They're fine."

"Has either of them met your new friend?"

Kimberly smiled. She knew that if she said yes, that would mean her friend was from New York. That would also mean that her mother would question the heck out of Brittany and Mia the next time she spoke with them.

"Yeah, they've met my friend."

"This friend of yours, the one who knows these big name designers, is he your new boyfriend?" Marjorie asked. She was tired of beating around the bush.

"You could say that."

"Oh, you have a new boyfriend?" Marjorie said, becoming very animated. "When were you going to tell us about him?"

Kimberly shrugged.

"You hear that, Thornton?" Marjorie shouted into the family room. "Your daughter has a new boyfriend."

"That's wonderful, dear," Thornton shouted back, while not peering up from his newspapers.

"That is *not* wonderful!" Marjorie declared. "She wasn't even going to tell us about him!"

"I was going to tell you about him," Kim said.

"When? Next month? Next year? When?"

"When the time was right."

"When the time was *right*?" Marjorie recoiled. She mixed her cornbread, and slammed the dish into her stainless steel Wolf oven. "Did you even tell him about us, or does he think you're an orphan?"

Kimberly exhaled and rolled her eyes.

"And you don't know what this young man does for a living?" Marjorie asked.

"Yes, he's an executive in the fashion industry."

"An executive," Marjorie said tartly. She pursed her lips together. "In the fashion industry. And who does this executive work for?"

"He works for Vespasian."

"Vespasian?" Marjorie nodded. "Impressive.

And how long have you been seeing this young man? Wait, he is a *young* man, isn't he?"

"Yes, mother," Kim said, exhaling forcibly again. "He and I are about the same age. And we've been seeing one another for a while."

"Does this young executive have a name?"

"Sterling. His name is Sterling."

"Sterling," Marjorie said nodding. "At least his parents gave him a sensible name. And what is Mr. Sterling's last name?"

"Williams."

"Sterling Williams," Marjorie said, again pursing her lips. "And when will we get the pleasure of meeting Mr. Williams?"

Kimberly shrugged.

"Oh, that's reassuring. You mean to tell me that you have no plans for how or when you were going to introduce your boyfriend to your parents?"

"I mean, I hadn't thought about it."

"I guess we're not that important to you."

Kimberly threw her head back in frustration. If it was one thing she hated more than anything else, it was her mother's guilt trips. "You can meet him!"

"No, don't do us any special favors," Marjorie told her. "We'll just have to be content with your sister's fiancée."

"Fiancee?"

"Yes, her *fiancée*," Marjorie repeated. "If you would call more often you would know what is going on in your family."

"I see you every Sunday!" Kimberly told her.

"Not *every* Sunday. Nevertheless, I am pleased to announce that your sister, and her long time boyfriend, Dr. Craig Andrew Phelps III, have become engaged. Another doctor in the family."

"Whoopee."

"Whoopee? Let's see. We'll have your father, your two uncles, your five cousins, your sister, her fiancée. And then we'll have you and your fiancée. Christmas dinner will consist of conversations about breathtaking medical research, and what Paris Hilton was wearing at some awards show."

Kimberly exhaled, and shook her head. She was defeated. Her mother had once again made her feel lower than low.

"I think the Paris Hilton conversation is going to be a lot more interesting!" Thornton shouted from the family room.

Kimberly smiled. Her father always made her feel better.

"Oh, *shut up, Thornton!*" Marjorie shouted.

Chapter Sixteen

"She just has a way of making me feel insignificant," Kimberly said sadly. "She lays this guilt trip on me about not being a doctor, about not marrying a doctor, about not going to grad school. I just feel like a miserable failure."

"You're not a miserable failure, Kim," Sterling told her. "You have a great job, a great life, and a wonderful boyfriend."

Kimberly laughed. "Two out of three ain't bad."

"What, you don't have a great job?" Sterling asked, lifting an eyebrow.

The two of them strolled along the cobble stone street, taking in the sights and sounds of a mild Martha's Vineyard evening.

Kim smiled, and the smile quickly bled from her face. "I just don't know what I can do to please that woman, short of going to medical school."

"You're a grown woman, Kimberly," Sterling told her. "You have your own life to live. Love your mother, honor her, cherish her, but live your own life."

"I know," Kim nodded. "What you're saying is true, but still. I've always looked up to her, and looked to her for guidance. Her opinion matters to me."

"Your mother's opinion *should* matter," Sterling said. "But take them for what they're worth. Don't let anyone tear you down."

Kimberly exhaled, stopped, and examined a nearby storefront window. "She just loved throwing it in my face that my sister was getting married."

"That's good news," Sterling told her. "Why would that bother you?"

"It doesn't bother me," Kim said, breathing out forcibly. "I'm happy for my sister. It's just that my mother relished throwing it in my face."

"Throwing what in your face?"

"The fact that my sister has found someone and I'm still single."

"You've found someone too," Sterling said softly. "You've found me. We've found each other."

Kimberly shook her head and folded her arms.

"Yeah, but the truth be known, to them we don't even count."

"We don't count?" Sterling recoiled. "We *always* count. Who says that they get to decide who counts? Since when did they get to decide our self esteem?"

"Sterling, in their world, we don't matter," Kimberly explained. "My mother, and her black doctor crowd. In their world, you can be the biggest investor on Wall Street, or a partner at the biggest law firm in New York, and you'll barely register."

"Kimberly, what does it matter if we don't fit into their world?" Sterling asked. "We're out to build a world of our own."

"That's easy for you to say, Sterling. This is my mother, and these are the people I grew up around. I don't want to be alienated from them."

Sterling took Kimberly's hand into his. "And I don't want to see you torn down. You're an exceptional woman. Sure, I'll go with you and meet your parents. But I won't sit silent and let anyone insult you or tell you that you aren't special. You are a phenomenal woman, Kimberly Neal."

Tears fell from Kimberly's eyes. She lifted Sterling's strong hands to her lips and kissed them. He was a healer, like her father. A man who built people up, instead of tearing them down. He was a good man, who had just proven that he would be there to lift her up when she was down.

"Come on, this is supposed to be a shopping trip," Sterling told her, nodding toward a nearby store.

Sterling and Kim ventured into the store, realizing after entering, that it was an expensive boutique that catered to Martha's Vinyard's super rich. After examining only two price tags, Kim spun on her heels toward the door.

"Let's get out of here!"

"What?" Sterling asked, turning his palms up.

"You see these prices?" Kimberly asked. "I can't afford anything in here!"

"I can," Sterling told her.

Kim shook her head. "I can't let you buy me anything from here, Sterling. I appreciate the gesture, but…"

Sterling clasped her hand and pulled her back inside. Kimberly shook her head, and reluctantly continued to browse. Sterling lifted a pair of heels on display.

"Cute!" Kimberly told him. She took the heels and examined the tag. "These are Manolos, and they are thirteen hundred bucks!"

"May I help you find something?" the saleswoman asked.

"We'll take these shoes in a size..." Sterling peered down at Kimberly's feet. "Seven?"

"Wow, you're good!" Kim said with a smile. "But, Sterling, I can't accept those shoes."

"You're right," Sterling told her. "How could you accept a pair of shoes, without a dress to match?"

"Sterling!"

Sterling whirled, and spotted a dress on display across the room. He rushed to it, and Kimberly raced behind him.

"This is a Louis Vuitton original," Kimberly told him.

Sterling examined the black and copper chiffon layered crinoline dress. "This is good."

Kimberly lifted the tag. "This is *fourteen thousand dollars*!"

"This matches those Manolo Blahnik heels I just bought you."

"Sterling, no!"

Sterling handed the saleswoman his black American Express card, and a business card with his Martha's Vinyard address on it. "Have it delivered this evening, please."

"Very good, sir!" she said, bowing her head slightly. She ran his card through her verification machine, and then handed it back to him.

Sterling and Kim headed out of the store and continued their leisurely stroll down the avenue.

"Sterling, I can't accept that dress," Kim told him.

"That dress is a done deal," Sterling told her. "If I can't buy things for my girlfriend, then this relationship sucks."

Kim laughed. "You can buy me things, just not things that cost as much as a small economy car."

Sterling pulled her close. "You told me about your mother's hopes and aspirations for you. What about your own dreams?"

"My dreams?"

"Yeah, tell me about *your* dreams. What do you want to do with your life?"

"Ideally, I would love to have my own fashion line. I love to design clothes. Give me a pencil, and a blank tablet, and I'm good."

"You have real talent."

"You think so?"

"I know so. I really like your designs. In fact, I want to show them to some people over at

Vespasian, with your permission of course."

"Vespasian?" Kim shook her head. "I don't think I'm ready for that."

"I think you are."

"Sterling, in that show in New Orleans, Vespasian showed designs that were light years ahead of everyone else. It was like art gliding down the runway. And in the Hamptons, the Geisha and Yakuza themes were out of this world. I can't create like that. That's on a whole other level."

"Kim, I've seen your designs!" Sterling said forcefully. "You're right there! You just have to believe in yourself."

Kim exhaled.

"You downplay your talent, you allow your mother to beat up on your career, you allow your boss to beat up on your achievements. You have to get out of that downtrodden mentality and realize how wonderful you are."

Kim caressed the side of Sterling's face. "Thank you."

"No need to thank me," Sterling told her. "I'm just telling the truth. You're smart, sharp, hard working, and talented. You can put a fashion line together. I can help you."

"You'd be willing to help me?"

"Of course."

Kim turned and hugged him.

"As a matter of fact, let me show your designs to some of my people at Vespasian."

Reluctantly, Kim nodded.

"Great. You're on your way. You could be the next Caroline Herrera, or Miuccia Prada, or Coco Chanel."

"Get out of here!"

"You can do anything," Sterling said sternly. He pulled her close, and she wrapped her arms around him. The two kissed passionately for several moments. "You want to go for a walk along the beach?"

"First, let's go back to your beach house so that I can change."

"Change?" Sterling held her arm up and examined her. "You look fantastic."

"I want to put on my two piece, and grab my sandals. I have some cute Ferragamo sandals that I have been dying to wear."

Sterling laughed. "Women."

"You're going to love my Dad," Kim told him. "He says that same thing all the time. You two are soul mates."

"Yeah? Then maybe I should be dating him."

"And leave me with my mother?" Kim lifted an eyebrow. "I don't think so!"

She and Sterling shared a long laugh. His laughter abated, when the glare of the Sun reflected off of an object in a shop window.

"That is gorgeous!"

Kim turned to see what he was talking about. It was a diamond tennis bracelet that sparkled like the North Star.

"C'mon," Sterling told her, heading into the shop.

Kim paused, and examined the sign above the door. It was Bulgari. "Sterling!"

Before she could stop him, his black American Express Card was in the hands of an extremely happy salesman.

Chapter Seventeen

"House of Dereon?" Laquisha called out, as she went through the various orders her sales executives were able to secure. "Joseph Abboud? Givenchy? Savile Row? Jimmy Choo? Kenneth Cole? I have three full time ad executives, and during three of the biggest fashion events of the year, they were able to secure six sales between the three of them?"

"I worked my ass off for that Givenchy sale!" Pamela told her.

"This is bullshit!" Laquisha shouted, tossing the orders across the room.

"Laquisha!" Kimberly shouted.

"Bulllshit! Bullshit! Bullshit!" Laquisha told them. "I am tired of the excuses, and of carrying dead weight around here! All I get is fucking excuses. Excuses from my writers, excuses from my photographers, excuses from production, excuses from marketing, excuses from copy, excuses until my *ass* hurts!"

"I've worked my ass off for you, Laquisha!" Dawn shouted. "I'm down to four hours of sleep per night during deadline week! My blood pressure is sky high, my cholesterol is out of whack, I'm finding gray hair in my brush, and it's all because of this stressful ass job!"

"Well you don't have to worry about those things anymore, Dawn!" Laquisha shouted. "Have your desk cleared out by the end of business today!"

"You can't fire me, because I quit!" Dawn shouted back. "You can take your little production manager position and stick it up your fat black ass!"

"Bitch, you can eat my cunt!" Laquisha shouted.

"Oh my goodness!" Tina gasped.

"You're fired too!" Laquisha told Tina.

Tina gasped again. "Laquisha!"

"Laquisha my ass! You're the marketing manager, and marketing has been in the dumps for months!"

"But, Laquisha!" Tina begged.

"Don't beg this bitch!" Dawn shouted. "Let's go, Tina!"

Tina rose from her seat.

"And when you hoes see my so-called *business manager*, you can tell her that her ass is fired too!" Laquisha shouted.

Tina and Dawn stormed out of Laquisha's office, slamming the door behind them.

"Anybody else want to follow those two?" Laquisha said, peering around the room.

Silence.

"Good! But now hear this!" Laquisha told them. "This is the captain speaking. We are getting this ship together. Any of you mother fuckers want overboard, then now is the time to jump ship. Also hear this. You will be thrown overboard if your shit ain't tight. Ad execs, that *especially* means you! We need to generate more ad revenue. You have exactly one week to bring in two new clients. And then I want at least one new client a week from each of you, plus your renewals. So, let's make sure we all understand one another. You are all on probation as of now. You have exactly one week, to keep your job. Now, you can all get the fuck out of my office."

*****

"Hello?"

"Sterling?"

"Yeah, it's me. Hey, sweety, how are you doing?"

"Not good," Kimberly exhaled.

"What's the matter?"

"I'm going to have to cancel our lunch date today."

"Why?"

"Work," Kimberly said, breathing out forcibly. "My boss is on our ass today."

"What else is new?"

"No, this time it's really bad. I have to make a sell between now and Friday, in order to keep my job."

"Yikes."

"I know. Sucks right?"

"Big time," Sterling told her. "Hey, you ever think about changing jobs?"

"Yeah, like right after today's meeting," Kim laughed. "I may *have* to find another job."

"Ever think about coming over to Vespasian?"

"Come on, Sterling? As what?"

"As a designer."

"Yeah, right!"

"I'm serious. Come on over, show us what you can do, and work your way into creating your own line under Vespasian. It's what you wanted to do, right? You wanted your own line."

"Well, yeah. But I wanted my own, not a line under someone else's line. Besides, it's really sweet of you, Sterling, but it wouldn't be right."

"What do you mean, be *right*?"

"*Hello?* You're my boyfriend."

"So?"

"So, I don't want my boyfriend to have to give me a job. You're an executive, I would be a newbie designer, hired on your recommendation. Everyone at the company would automatically hate me, and everyone in the fashion community would assume that I only got the job because of you."

"Forget what everyone else would think."

"Easy for you to say, because you wouldn't have to deal with it. When I start designing clothes, I want to get where I am, because of my own merit, not because of who I'm screwing."

"That's bullshit!" Sterling told her. "Your designs are great, Kim. You're very talented."

"Talented enough to get looked at by Vespasian had you not been there? Would Gucci look at my designs? What about Donna Karen?

What about Chanel?"

"I don't know what they would do, but I do know that the consensus here at Vespasian, is that you have a lot of talent and a lot of potential."

"Sterling, I appreciate it. This is just something that I have to do on my own. I have to know that it was my talent that opened the door for me, and not my tail."

"The offer remains on the table," Sterling told her.

"Thank you."

"Now, as your boyfriend, I'll just shut up and listen."

"Tonight," Kimberly told him. "I'll need those big strong shoulders to cry on tonight. Right now, I have to get busy and beat the bushes for a sale."

"Gotcha," Sterling told her. "Talk to you later."

"Bye."

"Bye," Sterling said, hanging up his telephone. He pressed the button on his speaker phone, summoning his secretary. She appeared almost instantaneously.

"Yes, sir?" she asked, opening his office door.

"Marlena, I want you to get with marketing,

and have Gil call over to Mocha Magazine and ask to speak to Kimberly Neal. Have him take out a full year's worth of advertising. Nothing special, maybe a page per issue, no more than three. We can start with the new reversible bags for now, and then we'll do something with our upcoming fall line later. Have him do the reversible bags, some of our new women's line, things like that. But it's really important that he deal with Kimberly Neal *only*. Got that?"

Marlena nodded as she scribbled the last few lines on her notepad. "Kimberly Neal only. Got it."

"That's it."

Marlena nodded and breezed out of the office. Sterling's telephone rang again.

"Hello?"

"Hey, Dad."

"Third! My main man! What's happening?"

"Are you going to come to my football game this weekend?

"I wouldn't miss it for the world!"

"I need some new football cleats," Third told him. "And a mouthpiece."

"I will pick it up today."

"Can I go with you, Dad?"

"You certainly can. I'll pick you up on my

way home from work if your mother says that it's okay. Where is your mom at?"

"She's right here."

"Let me speak to her."

"Hello?"

"Hey, Carmela."

"Hi, Sterling."

"How've you been?"

"I'm fine, and you?"

"Moving forward."

"That's always a good thing. Your son in playing for the Junior Falcons this year."

"He was just telling me that he needs new cleats," Sterling said. "I told him that I'll get them today, and he asked if he could come along. I guess he wants to pick them out or something. I just wanted to check with you and see if it was okay if I picked him up and took him with me."

Carmela exhaled into the telephone. "I guess. What time are you going to have him back? It is a school night."

"We're going to grab the cleats and whatever else he needs from the sporting goods store, maybe pick up something to eat, and I promise I'll bring him right home."

"Third, do you have homework?"

"No, Mom."

"Sterling, you have him home no later than eight thirty."

"Thanks, Carmela."

"Bye."

"Bye."

Chapter Eighteen

The Millennium Club was one of Manhattan's trendiest restaurants. Paris Hilton could be seen dining there at least once a week. Diddy dined there regularly, as did Jay Z. New York Giants, Jets, Yankees, Dodgers, and Knicks could be seen there throughout the week. It was a place where the hottest entertainers, fashion designers, actors, and athletes gravitated. It was a place to be seen in. A place where the line stretched outside of the building and down the sidewalk for the ordinary patrons, and where reservations were required well in advance for a Friday or Saturday night dining experience. It was the place where Vespasian maintained its very own table within the restaurant's VIP section.

"I can't believe you were able to get us in here!" Mia shouted over the restaurants loud stereo system.

"This is Vespasian's table!" Kim shouted. "Sterling hooked it up for us!"

Brittany raised her glass of Krug. "Kudos to Sterling!"

"Who's Sterling?" David asked.

"He's Kim's new boyfriend," Shaun told him.

"Kim has a new flame, huh?" David asked, smiling at her.

"Be nice," Kim told him.

"Yeah, or I'll deck you!" Brittany told her boyfriend.

David feigned innocence. "Me? I'm always nice!"

Mia leaned over and kissed Shaun. "You be nice too!"

"You mean we can't give him the third degree?" Shaun asked.

"Yeah, we have to find out his intentions," David added.

"Make sure they're honorable," Shaun smiled.

"Speaking of honorable, did you guys catch the debates last night?" Mia asked.

"I saw a piece of it," Kim told her.

Shaun exhaled and shifted his gaze toward the ceiling. "Please, don't get her started."

"That was the most dishonorable,

disingenuous pack of lies that I've ever heard!" Mia told them.

"I'm not sure what to make of her," Brittany said.

"Your parents know the Congresswoman, don't they?" David asked.

Brittany nodded. "And they know Romney as well. Mom absolutely adores Sarah Palin."

"I'm setting your mom's tires on flat!" Mia huffed.

"She'll just take one of the other Rolls," David smiled.

"Funny," Brittany said sarcastically.

"The nerve of them!" Mia shouted. "Three years ago they thought that they'd have my vote, just because their VP nominee was a woman! Massive fail! Hillary Clinton she is *not*! She's Pat Buchanan in heels. Strictly anti-abortion, even in cases of rape or incest. She's pro guns, a hunter, a Bambi killer for Christ sakes! She's a right wing religious nut. She's a lifetime member of the NRA! She's for drilling in the Artic National Wildlife Preserve! And now, they have this Paul Ryan character, and his inhumane budget!"

"Calm down," Shaun told her. "She's not running, remember?"

"Calm down?" Mia asked, turning her palms up. "When is it time to get nervous? When the Wildlife Preserve has been turned into one big gas station? When the polar ice cap has completely melted? When carbon dioxide from fossil fuels has poisoned all of our air and water? Lipstick and high heels doesn't make the Republican agenda any easier to swallow. Snooping on me and eroding my civil liberties is still a violation of my Constitutional Rights, whether it's done by Dick Cheney, or by the former Ms. Alaska runner up. And then, this Ryan budget is going to destroy every single social and educational program in existence! And then, the vaginal probes! The union busting! Ending Obamacare!"

"Tell us how you really feel," Brittany laughed.

"I just hope that women don't ever fall for that crap!" Mia said. "Sure, she's a woman, but she doesn't stand for anything that we stand for. She wants to take away our right to chose, but no one took away her right to chose. She's pro life, but pro death penalty, which is bullshit. She claims that she took on the good old boys, but she goes hunting with them!"

"She's not running this time," Brittany

reminded her. "It's Romney Ryan now, remember?"

"We all know you work for the Obama campaign," Shaun told her.

"You're damn right I do," Mia said. "And we all should be. This election is the biggest election of our time. The mortgage crises is still destroying American families, our economy is still in ruins, gas prices are still through the roof, the planet is in peril, terrorist are regrouping in Afghanistan, worker's unions are under assault, and our civil liberties are being eroded here at home, women's rights are under assault, and so is health care. We have to make the right decision in this election!"

"Mia, please don't run Sterling off with your political tirade," Kim begged.

"Don't tell me that Sterling is a Republican!" Brittany asked with a smile.

"*You are!*" Kim told her.

"My *parents* are," Brittany corrected.

"And you're not?" Shaun asked.

"I'm a new generation of the party," Brittany told them.

"Yeah, we're Republicans," David said, coming to his girlfriend's defense. "But we believe in a woman's right to choose. We don't believe in the death penalty, and we don't believe that government should spy on its citizens."

"And we do believe in global warming, and believe in saving the environment," Brittany added.

"And I'm a doctor, so naturally I'm not big on creationism," David told them. "And as a medical professional, I detest guns."

"So, on what issues do you agree with your party?" Shaun asked.

"Less government, lower taxes," David started.

"Yes, we're fiscal conservatives," Brittany told them.

"Ah, don't-mess-with-my-money Republicans!" Shaun laughed.

The others around the table joined in the laughter.

"You'll tolerate a lot of the liberal social policies, as long as they don't touch the bank account," Kim said laughing.

"Here comes Mr. Sterling!" Mia announced.

Kim rose from the table and hugged Sterling when he walked up. "Guys, this is Sterling."

Nods and greetings went around the table.

"Sterling, this is Mia," Kim said. Sterling and Mia shook hands. "This is Brittany."

"Good to meet you," Brittany said, shaking

hands with Sterling.

"This is Brittany's boyfriend, David." Kim said, introducing them. Sterling and David shook hands. "And this is Shaun, Mia's boyfriend."

"Good to meet you," Shaun told Sterling as they shook hands.

Sterling seated himself. "So, how have you been enjoying yourselves?"

"Fantastic!" Kim said.

"I can't believe this place!" Mia told him. "It's everything that people said it was!"

"So, Sterling, let's hear your opinion on the upcoming elections," Mia told him.

"I don't do politics when I'm with friends," Sterling told her.

"Why not?" Shaun asked.

"Yeah, that's the best time to do politics," Mia said.

"Friendship and political opinions, don't always mix," Sterling answered.

"I'll bet you he's a Republican," Mia said, teasing.

"Hey, y'all leave my man alone!" Kim told them.

"Leave him alone?" Brittany laughed. "We haven't even gotten started with him yet!"

"Yeah," David chimed in. "We haven't even asked him what his intentions are."

Sterling laughed.

"I'm sorry, baby," Kim told him.

"That's okay," Sterling said, waving off her apology. "I'm glad that you have friends who look out for you."

"So, Sterling, what *are* your intentions?" Brittany asked.

"What do you think about the direction this country is going in?" Mia asked.

"Are you a Republican, Sterling?" Shaun asked.

"What's wrong with being a Republican?" David asked Shaun.

"Woah, calm down, guys," Kimberly said, holding up her hands. "You can question him, but let's not turn this into the Spanish Inquisition."

"Let's see," Sterling said, placing his hand beneath his chin. "My intentions are to be a loving, supportive, caring boyfriend to Kim. I think that this is the greatest country in the world, but I also think that we can do better. No, I'm not a Republican. I consider myself more of an Independent. And yes, Mia. I'm supporting Obama in this election, even though I really need those

Bush tax cuts to be permanent. Obama wants to increase taxes on the rich, and I'm rich. But, if I have to pay a little more in order to insure that poor people in this country have health care, and that we save the planet, then I'm willing to do that."

"Wow, an undercover Republican who's willing to take a hit to his wallet!" Shaun said, teasing. "Unlike some other Republicans at the table, who shall remain nameless."

"Brittany and David!" the group said in unison. Everyone around the table burst into laughter.

"Sorry, Sterling, it's a little inside joke," Kim explained. "Brittany's last name is Sherwood, as in Sherwood Hotels. And David's last name is Phillips, as in Phillips Petroleum. They come from old money, White, Anglo-Saxon, Protestant, East Coast establishment Republican families."

"And Mia never lets us forget it," David added.

"Don't be embarrassed about your trust funds now," Mia smiled.

"David is also a doctor," Brittany said. "He's earning his way through life by helping heal people."

"Okay, so he's a good Republican WASP!"

Mia said, smiling.

"Speaking of doctors, guess who I ran into the other day," Shaun said.

"Who?" Brittany asked.

"John," Shaun said.

Mia elbowed him under the table.

"What?" Shaun asked, turning his palms up.

Mia nodded toward Sterling.

"That's okay," Sterling reassured her. "I know about John. I'm not insecure."

"It's just bad etiquette to talk about the old boyfriend when the new boyfriend is sitting right in front of your face!" Brittany said through clenched teeth.

"I was just saying," Shaun said. "He was telling me that he's getting married. Did you guys know?"

"Yes, we knew!" Mia said, rolling her eyes.

"I got an invitation," David said.

"He said that mine was in the mail," Shaun told them. "Did you get an invitation?"

"Yes!" Brittany snapped.

"Did you?" Shaun asked Kim.

Kim turned her head and stared across the room. "Yeah."

"Well, it's the elephant in the room," Shaun

said. "We might as well talk about it. Who's going?"

"Shaun!" Mia said, punching him in his chest.

"What?" Shaun asked.

"You're an idiot," David told him.

"It's okay," Sterling told them.

"I have to go, he's a colleague, remember?" David said.

"I have to go with David as his date," Brittany said.

"Same with me and Mia," Shaun said. He turned toward Kim.

"My parents are going," Kim said. "He also sent me an invitation to my parent's home."

Sterling turned toward Kim. "I understand. If you want to go, I won't be upset with you."

"I don't know," Kim said, exhaling. "If I was to go, it would be for all the wrong reasons."

"Like what?" Sterling asked.

"To see this bi... young lady that he's marrying," Kim said, catching herself.

"I heard that she looks young," Brittany said.

"Like a high school pop tart!" Mia said. "That boy is robbing the cradle!"

Laughter went around the table.

"I would mainly go," Kim said solemnly. "To

show that bastard that he didn't break me."

Chapter Nineteen

Sterling leaned back in his chair and propped his feet up onto his desk.

"You don't have to thank me, Kim," He said, adjusting the telephone next to his ear. "Vespasian was planning on launching its new bags with a vigorous ad campaign anyway. I just told the marketing department who to contact over at Mocha."

"Yeah, I'm sure, Sterling," Kim said. "You can't keep on doing this."

"Doing what?"

"Coming to my rescue."

"What are you talking about?" Sterling asked. "I work for a fashion house, you work for a fashion magazine. Fashion houses advertise in fashion magazines. What's unusual about that? Our companies do business together all the time. This time, I happened to know one of the ad execs, and told someone in marketing, that executive's name. Nothing wrong with that."

"You're out of this world, you know that?"

"I've been told that before."

"So, are you going to go with me?"

"With you? Where?"

"To John's wedding," she asked nervously.

"You want to take your new boyfriend, to your ex-boyfriend's wedding?" Sterling asked.

"Yeah."

"That's freaky."

Kim laughed. "I know on the surface it sounds a little weird, but I need your support."

"My support?" Sterling asked. "And this is not just to show dude that you have someone too?"

"In a way it is. I do want to show him that I've moved on."

"Well, if you feel that you have to show him that you've moved on, then that means you really haven't moved on. Why do you need to show him anything? Why does he still even matter?"

"Sterling, you don't know what I went through," Kim said softly. "You don't know what they tried to do to me."

"They? Who is they?"

"John, his family, a lot of people who I thought

were my friends," Kim explained. "They all turned on me. They went out of their way to make life miserable for me. They wanted to break me. They wanted to make me bow down, and accept all of the shit John was putting me through. They took me off of all their little guest lists, I was uninvited from parties and other social events, and I was basically snubbed in public. I have to walk in that place with my head held high, and show them all that I'm still here! I want to walk in there and show them that they didn't break me."

"So, what happened between you two?" Sterling asked.

"I couldn't take his stepping out on me with his baby mommas," Kim explained. "And I couldn't deal with all of the drama that they kept bringing into our relationship. It was always something with them. It really got out of control when they started slashing my tires and breaking my windows and calling my job. After that, I vowed that I would never again date a man with a kid. No more baby momma drama for me."

Sterling went silent.

"Hey, my boss is calling me," Kim told him. "I'll talk to you later. Think about going to the wedding with me, please. We have a few weeks before you have to decide."

"Okay, baby," Sterling said softly. "I'll talk to you later."

"Bye."

"Bye."

Sterling's office door swung open.

"We're in deep shit!" Wilson told him, slinging a brown leather purse onto Sterling's desk.

"What's this?" Sterling said, glancing over the bag. "This is nice!"

"That's why we're up shit creek!" Wilson told him. "It isn't ours."

"Oh," Sterling sat up in his seat.

"Please allow me to present Ralph Lauren's brand new Ricky Bag," Wilson said. "A three thousand eight hundred and fifty dollar nod to sheer luxury. Rich women are going to go crazy over this thing. There is going to be a line of BMWs and Mercedes two miles long outside of every Saks Fifth Avenue, and Neiman Marcus in the country. We are in trouble."

Sterling lifted the saddle colored leather bag and examined it carefully. "Hmmm. Gold hardware, great structure, sophisticated, elegant, great stitching, versatile."

"Critics are calling it this season's 'it' bag,"

Wilson told him.

"We have a similar bag coming out," Sterling told him.

"Yeah, but our bag is eighteen hundred dollars," Wilson pointed out. "If they put out a bag that's almost four grand, and we put out a bag that's almost two grand, and they both look similar, it makes our bag look like a cheap knock off. Remember the Louis Vuitton slash Dooney and Burke fiasco? It will belittle our whole line. Our whole company."

"So what do we do? Raise the price on our bag by two grand?"

"That may be the only thing we *can* do," Wilson told him. "Our leather is just as thick, we're using real gold hardware, thick triple stitching, top of the line hides, we have great structure, everything. We could legitimately sell our bags for the same price."

"And that would mean?"

"That women would have to decide between a Ralph Lauren or a Vespasian bag, or they would have to buy both."

"Buy both?" Sterling asked, lifting an eyebrow. "That's almost eight thousand dollars for two leather purses that look exactly the same."

"These are extremely rich women that these bags are targeting. They can afford both. But that is not our only problem."

Sterling leaned back and exhaled. "What's the really bad news?"

"Well, we designed our brown leather bag to go hand in hand with our multi-color," Wilson explained. They are virtually the same bags, but the brown bag was to appeal to either older, or more conservative women, or women who wanted a more sophisticated bag for more sophisticated occasions. We had anticipated a lot of women springing for both bags, with the multi-color being an everyday bag. Our marketing department also felt that they could be paired as mother-daughter sets, with the multi-color being the daughter's bag. Well, if we move that bag upscale, then we'll have nothing to pair with our multi-color."

"So, we'll have to design another bag to go with the multi-color?" Sterling asked.

"That's the best solution. I've already got the designers working on it. Now, this leaves us with our third problem. Our multi-color was supposed to be the 'it' bag this season. Going up against this new Ralph Lauren bag, and our own 'Ricky Bag', is going to steal our multi-color's thunder."

"Our bag is reversible, and the V's glow in the dark," Sterling pointed out. "We have the teen and young adult market on lock. They are the ones who are going to determine the year's 'it' bag, not the critics. Let's go with what we have, keep the price the same for our 'Ricky Bag', and bring out a new design to compete with their 'Ricky Bag'. Did you see the new design that Gianna sent over from Italy?"

"Which one?"

"That brown leather 'Mummy Bag' that she did," Sterling told him. "That thing is cold! When I saw it, my mouth fell open."

"I haven't seen it," Wilson told him.

"It's gorgeous. It's toffee colored leather, with two diagonal stitches running down the sides, but the stitching is hidden in the seams. It looks like three thick pieces of leather sewn together, with diagonal stitching. The gold clasp up top is hidden behind a thick leather flap that goes down one side of the bag, and buttons into a recessed section beneath the bag, so it sits flush at the bottom. The leather flap corresponds with the center section of the bag, so it maintains that three piece look. I mean, that thing is awesome. I was definitely thinking of pricing that bag between four to six thousand dollars."

Wilson placed his hand beneath his chin and smiled. "Hmmmm. The Mummy Bag. I like it. In fact, I love it. We're going to blow them out of the water."

"Call Italy, get the ball rolling. Get the CAD files to the shop and have them manufacture a few of them for market testing."

Wilson nodded. "I'll get right on it."

*****

Kimberly knocked on her boss's door.

"In!" Laquisha shouted.

Kimberly pushed open the door and stepped inside. "You wanted to see me??"

Laquisha nodded. "Yeah. Good work on landing the Vespasian ad. I knew that you could do it. I also got a phone call from Pinault-Printemps-Redoute while you were out. They want to take out an advertisement with you. Apparently your little trip to New Orleans paid off quite well."

"Pinault-Printemps-Redoute?" Kimberly asked, confused.

"You don't even know who you're selling too?" Laquisha asked. "Gucci! It's Gucci's parent company!"

Sterling! It had to be Sterling, Kimberly thought. He was at it again.

"That's two big ones in a row," Laquisha told her. "I can't help but to say congratulations. This helps me solve a dilemma that I was facing. I was wondering who to send to The Magic Show as the lead ad executive, but now that decision is easy."

Kimberly couldn't help the smile that came across her face.

"I'm sending you to the Magic Show as the head of our Advertising Department," Laquisha told her. "Consider it a trial. You do well, and I'll consider you for the permanent position of Advertising Manager."

Kimberly bounced up and down in her heels. "Oh, Laquisha! Thank you! Thank you! Thank you!"

Laquisha waved her off. "This is contingent on you continuing to bring in the type of clients you brought in this week."

"I won't let you down, Laquisha!" Kim said excitedly. "I promise!"

"Go to the Magic Show and get my money!"

Kimberly nodded. "Do the others know yet?"

Laquisha shook her head. "They're your team now, you tell them."

Kimberly nodded. It was the promotion that she had always dreamed of. She was now management, and surely her mother couldn't call her job a 'dead end' one now! She couldn't wait to tell her. And Sterling! She would call him as soon as she got back to her office. She was Advertising Manager at Mocha. You go girl, she told herself.

Chapter Twenty

The New York School For The Gifted And Talented was quickly becoming the premiere private academy on the East Coast. It was challenging old stalwarts like Exeter and Groton, particularly amongst New York's metropolitan residents. It was a lot closer, and the academics were on par or even better than those age old institutions. The New York Academy For The Gifted And Talented focused more on mathematics, science, and engineering than the traditional prep schools. If Groton and Exeter were the Harvard and Yale of prep schools, then NY Gifted and Talented was their MIT and Caltech equivalent. Students were encouraged to design their own software programs during the second semester of their freshman year. For engineering classes, they were taught to build their own computers, and then design a bridge, an airplane, or a building on that same operating system. They were taught to build and maintain entire networks by the end of the first semester of their junior year, and by the end of their senior year, were familiar with lasers, nanotechnology, biomedical science, and robotics.

NY Gifted and Talented was a school with a curriculum designed to produce doctors, scientist, and engineers, and it did so in impressive numbers. All of its students graduated, all of them went to college, with ninety percent of them going to Ivy League colleges. The remainder went to Oxford, Cambridge, United States Military Academies, Caltech, and Stanford. East Coast parents were taking notice.

The campus for Gifted and Talented was a sprawling two hundred acre beauty that was part nature preserve, part prep school campus. The school not only had its own bio science dome, but its own hanger, as well as a retired Boeing 707 for its engineering and aeronautical studies department. It also had its own group of elite scientist and doctors as teachers.

It was no secret that New York Gifted and Talented only hired Ph Ds. It was a sore point amongst many in the teaching profession. The teacher's union was particularly pissed, feeling that since the majority of its members lacked Ph Ds, that they were being looked upon as being inferior. The truth of the matter, was that they *were* looked upon that way by the school. NY Gifted and Talented's base pay for a teacher was over one hundred thousand dollars a year. This enabled them to pull in top flight staff, and also enabled them to charge parents a ludicrous amount for tuition. Fifty thousand dollars a year, plus books, plus uniforms, was the price of admission. Sterling paid this, and much more. In fact, Sterling's generosity was the reason that everyone was gathered at the school's convocation center on this day.

"It is in giving to the next generation, where we find our greatest service to humanity," the Headmaster said, speaking to the crowded auditorium. He adjusted his microphone, and peered out over the clapping crowd of wealthy and educated parents and faculty. "No gift is greater, no gift more precious, no gift more sacred, than the passing of knowledge from one generation to the next."

Again, the crowd clapped.

"We are gathered here today, to celebrate the

passing of knowledge, in the form of a library," the Headmaster continued. "A library that will serve this institution, and generations of future leaders, scientists, and medical doctors for many years to come."

Again those gathered applauded.

"The Sterling Barrington Williams III Library and Research Learning Center will be a five hundred thousand square foot monolith, dedicated to higher education," the Headmaster declared. "It will house not only our school's expanding collection of books and papers, but also our growing collection of original artwork, and our new computer learning center. It will also house our new bio-science laboratory. Today is a momentous occasion indeed. One that we have been looking forward to, since breaking ground on construction more than two years ago."

More applause.

"It is with great pleasure that I introduce to you, the man who made today possible," the Headmaster continued. "Mr. Sterling Williams!"

Sterling rose from his seat on the stage and walked to the microphone, where he shook hands with the Headmaster. The crowd's applause was thunderous. The Headmaster stepped from in front of the microphone podium, and motioned for Sterling to take over.

"Thank you," Sterling told the crowd, as he stepped in front of the microphone. "It is with great pleasure that I present to you, the Sterling Barrington Williams Library and Research Learning Center. It is my sincerest hope that this center will serve to enrich the minds of many generations of future leaders. From this center, my greatest hopes spring. Perhaps the seeds of a cure for cancer, or diabetes, or Alzheimer's disease will be planted in a young mind. From this center, perhaps the cure for spinal bifida, cerebral palsy, or many other chronic and debilitating diseases will be realized. Hope springs eternal, as a result of our faith in our young people. May this center be the well head for our hopes and dreams."

The Headmaster handed Sterling a giant pair of scissors, and the two of them turned toward a giant red ribbon that was tied to the building's double glass entrance doors.

A Catholic priest stepped forward and made the sign of the cross. "May the Lord bless this learning center, and all of the young men that it serves. May they go forward and do the Lord's work. May His Grace, and goodness, and mercy guide them, and follow them all the days of their lives."

The Headmaster waved his hand toward the ribbon, giving Sterling the signal to cut it. Sterling lifted the massive scissors and cut the giant ribbon to thunderous applause.

"And may I present, the center's namesake, and my inspiration," Sterling told the crowd. "My son, the love of my life, my hope, my dream, everything that was ever good, and pure, and decent about me. My son, Sterling Barrington Williams III!"

The audience applauded wildly as Third made his way up to the podium and hugged his dad.

"And now, a tour of our new library and learning center!" the Headmaster said proudly. He waved his hand toward the entrance, inviting the attendees inside.

"Sterling! Sterling!"

Sterling turned in the direction from which the voice came. It was Brittany's boyfriend.

"David, right?" Sterling asked.

"Yeah!" David said, shaking Sterling's hand. "Wow, nice library!"

"Thanks."

"Must have set you back a pretty penny,"

David told him.

"It did," Sterling said, running his hand over Third's waves. "But it was worth it."

"I had no idea that you were *the* Sterling Barrington Williams, CEO of Vespasian International," David told him. "I mean, Kim said you worked for Vespasian, but I had no idea that you were the CEO, Chairman, and majority shareholder. I don't want to sound like an asshole, but I always imagined Sterling Williams to be some old, rich, White guy. This is crazy! I'm impressed!"

"What brings you here today?" Sterling asked.

"I teach a couple of classes here," David told him.

"You're a physician."

"And they pay me very well to teach an anatomy and biology class here," David told him. "I had no idea that Third was your son. He's a very bright student. One of my best."

"Thank you."

"Wow, I just can't *believe* this," David said again. "*You're* Sterling Williams!"

"Yes, I am…"

David leaned in. "What does it feel like to be around all of those supermodels?"

Sterling laughed heartily. "My job is not like

that.   There's nothing glamorous about running Vespasian. It's just like any other CEO job. Endless meetings, a telephone glued to your ear, too many nights in hotels, and too much paperwork."

"C'mon, Sterling, you can't fool me!" David said nudging him. "I see the way all you clothing gurus are surrounded by gorgeous models all the time. You guys are the luckiest guys in the world. All the models, the Italian suits, the Ferraris, the fashion shows, the champagne, the exotic locations. That's the way to live."

Sterling laughed. "It's not all glitz and glamor, let me just say that."

David turned toward the building. "Well, let me just say this, you've put your money to good use with this library. My new office is going to be located here."

"Well, then I expect you to give a sizable donation to help fill the library with books."

"The dean has already hit me up for fifty grand," David smiled.

"Sterling!"

Sterling turned. It was Wilson.

"Great speech!" Wilson told him. "Hey, Third, how you doing, my man?"

"Good!" Third said, hi-fiving Wilson.

"Wilson, this is David," Sterling said, introducing the two.

"Good to meet you," Wilson said, exchanging handshakes.

"My pleasure," David told him.

"Sterling, I just talked to Italy," Wilson told him. "Gianna and Amerigo have already left for Vegas. They've sent all the clothes ahead by private carrier, and I've talked to Ford. We've got the models that we requested."

"Great," Sterling told him. "Did they give you a peak at what we're debuting this fall?"

"No," Wilson huffed. "They were under orders *not* to show anyone."

"Good. I want everyone surprised. Our fall lineup is going to take the fashion world by storm."

"And you're not even going to give me a hint?" Wilson asked.

Sterling shook his head slowly. "Let's just say, we're going to blow everyone out of the water. They are all going in one direction, and our new look is going to take us in a completely different direction."

"I guess that's good news. Now for the bad news," Wilson smiled. "You have to get out of here tomorrow morning."

231

"What?"

"The only flight the girls could get at this time."

"I need a private jet," Sterling said. "I knew that I should have commissioned one a long time ago."

"We'll take care of that this year," Wilson told him. "With the new lines, you'll really need one now. But in the meantime, you need to get packed and get ready to get out of here."

"Can I at least tour the building that I paid an arm and a leg for?" Sterling asked with a smile.

Wilson waved his arm toward the building in dramatic fashion and bowed slightly. "Your building, your highness."

"Thank you," Sterling smiled. He and Third walked into the building to began their tour.

Chapter Twenty One

The Magic Show was the premiere trade event for the international fashion industry. It was a place where over 20,000 product lines were displayed, and where some of the world's biggest fashion trends emerged. It was at Magic where Tommy Hilfiger first embraced the hip hop style, introducing oversized sweatshirts and baggy jeans. It was where Ralph Lauren introduced his iconic Polo Shirt, and where the world was first introduce to the bell bottomed jean. The Magic Show brought together international fashion giants, small boutique fashion houses, trade suppliers, distributors, designers, models, retailers, buyers, and numerous other industry insiders. It was the place where Hollywood and high fashion met to decide the new trends in the fashion world.

One of the most anticipated parts of Magic, were the fashion shows. It was in the main hall of the Las Vegas Convention Center, where tomorrow's trends were put on display. It was here, where industry insiders could make or break a designer's hard work for the year. A couple of nods from the right people could launch a designer or a new line into the stratosphere, while a couple of frowns or pursed lips could sink them into the abyss.

"There's my boyfriend!" Kim said, walking up behind Sterling.

Sterling turned and hugged her. "We're up next."

Kim could feel the tension in his body. "Nervous?"

"A little," Sterling told her. "This could make or break our season. We're going for a whole new look, and introducing a whole new line. This is going to be called The Vespasian Ivy *Collezione*."

"Vespasian Ivy *Collezione*?" Kim asked, trying to pronounce the words in proper Italian, while lifting an eyebrow.

Sterling nodded. "It brings together the world's of Italian high fashion, and Ivy League dress. Think nerdy, yet sophisticated. Think Oxford, meets Saville Row meets Milan. Think argyle and tweed, merged with fitted Italian suits."

"I'm having a hard time picturing this look,"

Kim told him. "I'm going to have to see it."

"Well, we're up next," Sterling said nervously.

Behind Sterling, Wilson paced back and forth nervously.

"And now, ladies and gentlemen," the announcer said, "Presenting Vespasian new fall line up. The Ivy *Collezione*!"

The first model that walked onto the stage was male. He wore a fitted Italian suit, with an argyle tie, matching argyle socks, and tortoise shell eyeglasses. He also had shell toe shoes, and an argyle sweater tied around his neck. His heavily moussed hair was messily styled around his head, while his walk was timid and nervous. He pulled off the Nerd in the tight Italian suit look perfectly.

The next model on the stage, wore a gray tweed blazer, gray Italian slacks, with matching argyle socks, tie, and pocket square. Again, the model wore tortoise shell frames, and had his moussed hair spiked into a nerdy do. He also had an argyle sweater tied around his waist. The crowd went wild.

The next model was a female. She wore a full length dress skirt, with a tweed blazer, a turtleneck sweater, tortoise shell glasses, argyle socks, and a pair of brown suede clogs. Her hair was pinned up, and she walked timidly down the runway carrying a brown suede book bag. Again, the look was a success.

Vespasian model after model made their way down the runway to thunderous applause.

"Looks like your fall line is a success," Kimberly said, hugging Sterling.

Gianna leaped into Sterling's arms after Kim was done with her hug. "They love it!"

"You and Amerigo did a fantastic job!" Sterling told her.

Wilson hugged Gianna, lifting her off of the floor and spinning her around. "Bravo! Fantastico!"

Hugs and congratulations went around the Vespasian staff.

"Sterling, wonderful job," said one gentleman, patting him on his back as he walked by.

"Thanks," Sterling told him. He turned toward Kimberly. "So, what did you think? Honestly."

"Honestly?" Kim said hesitating. "I thought that it was awesome! I can't believe you pulled that look off. It was very chic, very modern, yet classy. The blazers, the argyle, the Birkenstocks, the tweed, the tortoise frames, the shell toes, and wing tips, all blended together with Italian elements. It was crazy."

"Urkel meets Versace?"

"Yeah!" Kim nodded. "It was like blending two things that you would have never thought went together. Like a damn Reese's Peanut Buttercup. Who would have thought peanut butter and chocolate went together? I would have never imagined combining the elements that you combined in this show. It was fantastic. And those fitted Italian suits, those are to die for. Those alone are going to sell like crazy."

"Sterling, to your right!" Wilson told him.

Sterling peered over his right shoulder, to find two gentlemen lifting their champagne glasses in toast to him. He nodded in appreciation.

"Who is that?" Kim asked.

"That, my dear, is Alain and Gerard Wertheimer," Sterling told her.

"Wertheimer?"

"Chanel," Sterling explained. "Those gentlemen, own Chanel."

"There's Marc Jacobs talking to Tom Ford," Wilson whispered into Sterling's ear. "They're eating their hearts out!"

"I just received hugs from Alber Ebaz and

Michael Kors," Gianna told them.

"We did it, Sterling," Wilson said giddily. "We flipped the show on its head."

"Everyone was showing dark colors," Gianna pointed out. "Ugly, dark, floral patterns, and navy, forest green, and black. I knew that we should go with our basic browns, beiges, and tans, and mix them with tweeds and argyle patterns. Bringing in a New England look, with European flair was the right thing to do."

"And you were right," Sterling told her.

"We need you here full time, Gianna," Wilson told her.

Gianna shook her head. "Italy is my home. I can't imagine not living in Europe, and being able to take the train to France, Switzerland, and Germany. Not being able to go to Rome? Forget it!"

"You know that you've just won Designer of the Year by the Council of Fashion Designers of America?" Amerigo asked Sterling.

"How do you figure that?" Sterling asked.

"Everyone is talking about your show," Amerigo told him. "If you don't win it, then they are crazy. If I were you, I would quite America and go and live in Italy!"

"Calm down, Amerigo," Wilson said smiling

and placing his hand on Amerigo's shoulder. "But I do agree with you. Vespasian should win design house of the year. And you and Gianna should get designers of the year, male and female. Sterling should be asked to be president of the Council of Fashion Designers of America in the least."

"Okay, before you all plan the rest of my life, I'm going to hit the bar," Sterling told them. He held out his arm, and Kim clasped it. The two of them headed for the bar in another section of the massive convention center.

"When did you get into town?" Sterling asked.

"Late last night," Kimberly told him. "And you?"

"Yesterday morning."

"How was the Gucci party last night?"

"It was a blast," Sterling told her. "They always throw excellent parties. Plenty of champagne, A- list entertainment, plenty of celebrity star power, the works. Gucci pulls out all the stops when it comes to throwing big bashes for the industry."

"Who did they have for entertainment?"

"Wyclef, John Legend, Mary J. Blige, Eric Clapton, Elton John, and about half a dozen others."

"Wow! I'm sorry I missed that!"

"Mary was wearing Vespasian, and so was Kiesha Cole," Sterling said proudly. "I believe Eric was also."

"Congratulations on the show back there. You were a big hit."

"Thanks. I'm just glad that you showed up. I was a nervous wreck before you showed up."

"Oh, come on now, Sterling. You've done this a million times, so I know you couldn't have been *that* nervous."

"I was," Sterling nodded. "But you gave me strength, and confidence, like a good woman should."

"Are you going to start this again?"

"Start what?"

"All the compliments?" Kim smiled. "Making me feel good about myself?"

"You *should* feel good about yourself."

Kimberly nodded. "I do. I got a surprise for you too."

"Oh really?" Sterling asked, lifting an eyebrow. "A surprise for me? I like surprises. Cough it up." Sterling began feeling on Kim.

"Stop it!" Kim said, pushing his hand away. "It's not that type of surprise, silly!"

"I still want to feel on you though!" Sterling said, reaching for her again.

"Octopus!" Kim shouted, shoving his hands away again. "Can you control yourself?"

"Until when?"

"Until tonight," Kim said, giving him a seductive smile.

"I guess I'll have to wait then," Sterling told her. "So, what's the surprise?"

"I got a promotion."

"A promotion?" Sterling scooped her up into the air and twirled her around. "Baby, that's fantastic! I'm so proud of you! And happy for you too!"

"Thank you," Kim said gushing.

"We have to go out and celebrate!" Sterling said excitedly. "You pick a place."

Kimberly shrugged. "I don't know any places in Vegas."

"Don't worry about it. I'll have my secretary find us the finest restaurant in town, and make us reservations for tonight. We are going to celebrate big time!"

"I couldn't have done it without you," Kim told him.

"Yes you could have, and you would have."

"Sterling, you always talk about how I give you strength. Well, you give me that and much more. You're my inspiration. I get out of bed in the morning with a smile on my face because of you. Thank you so much. I thank the Man Upstairs everyday, for bringing you into my life."

"You and me both, baby," Sterling told her. He leaned in, and the two of them kissed passionately.

Chapter Twenty Two

"Happy Birthday, Brittany!" Mia shouted, as she entered the room carrying a massive white sheet cake.

"Okay, whose idea was it to put all of those candles on my cake?" Brittany asked.

"David's!" Kim said pointing.

Brittany punched her boyfriend in his shoulder.

"That's a gorgeous cake!" Kimberly declared.

"That thing can feed an army!" Shaun added.

"Awwww, thanks, guys!" Brittany said, peering around the room. "You guys are the best friends a girl could ever dream of having."

"You're worth it, Brit!" Kim said.

"Yeah, every bit of it!" Mia said, hugging Brittany.

The doorbell rang, and Kim raced to the door and opened it.

"Happy Birthday!" Kendall shouted, as she entered the apartment carrying a large present.

"Happy Birthday, girl!" Geri said, also entering the apartment with a large wrapped gift.

"Thanks, guys!" Brittany shouted from across the room.

"Presents are in the bedroom!" Kim said pointing. "You can just set them on the bed to get them out of the way for now."

Brittany's cousins, Anna, and Markova pushed the door open, just as Kimberly was about to close it.

"Happy Birthday!" they shouted in unison.

Kim pointed toward the bedroom. "Gifts in the bedroom."

Markova hugged Kim. "So good to see you."

"You look good, girl!" Kim replied. "Are you still with Ford?"

Markova nodded. "Have you seen my latest add for Cover Girl?"

"I saw that!" Kim said excitedly. She hugged Markova. "You looked drop dead gorgeous in that commercial. Your hair was to die for!"

"She looks rail thin!" Anna said of her sister. "They are starving her."

"You're not exactly a piglet yourself," Kim

said, examining Anna.

The girls were twins, born in Moscow, to a Russian mother. Brittany's uncle had met and married their mother while in graduate school at Oxford, and the twins had been born during his ambassadorship to Russian. Both of them had their mother's platinum blonde hair, baby blue eyes, and rail thin figure. They had pouting lips, a natural eyeliner, long blonde lashes, and perfectly trimmed eyebrows. They also had their father's last name of Sherwood, and all of his money, which translated into never having to lift a finger their enter lives. They had grown up in Europe and in the Hamptons, and had basically been born to be supermodels.

"I'm a two," Anna said defending herself. "This pretzel stick is a zero."

"A zero?" Kim asked Markova.

Markova smiled and nodded. "I have to maintain my figure."

The twins stalked off to the bedroom to place their gifts on the bed. Kimberly watched them and laughed, because they walked as if they were on a runway twenty four hours a day.

Mia lifted the remote and turned up the music. "Let Diddy get this party crunk!"

"Mia, you and the word *crunk*, do not go

together!" Brittany told her.

"I can use the word *crunk* if I feel like using the word *crunk*," Mia said. "What, the Asian bitch can't be down?"

The room burst into laughter.

Again the doorbell rang.

Kim opened the door, and to her surprise, it was Sterling, carrying a huge gift. She leaped into his arms. "Sterling!"

"Hey," he said, hugging her and trying to hold on to his gift. "Am I late?"

"No, you're right on time!" Mia shouted.

"Come on in here!" Brittany shouted. "Damn, girl, let the man breathe!"

"That must be a helluva gift!" David said smiling. He shook Sterling's hand.

"Yeah, open mine's first, so I won't be embarrassed!" Shaun added. "We know Mr. Vespasian here has brought something way out of our price range."

"Leave him alone!" Brittany said, taking Sterling's gift off of his hands.

"I couldn't believe it when David told me, man!" Shaun said, shaking Sterling's hand.

"Believe what?" Kim asked.

"You scored the mother lode with this one!"

Shaun told her.

"Yes, I did," Kim said, wrapping her arms around Sterling and peering up at him.

"I can't believe I'm cool with somebody famous," Shaun said.

"Famous?" Kim recoiled. Again she peered up at Sterling. "You're famous, Boo?"

Sterling shrugged.

Again the doorbell rang, and Kim opened it. More guests arrived. Soon, the party was in full swing. Guest were spread throughout Brittany's massive penthouse apartment. Sterling found himself in the kitchen near the blender, where several of the guys were making drinks.

"Taste this," David said, handing Sterling a glass.

"Blah!" Sterling said, wiping his mouth. "Too strong, and way too fruity. What the hell is this stuff?"

"It's my super strawberry daiquiri blend," David told him. "It's for the women."

"I can tell!" Sterling said laughing.

"What do all those supermodels drink?" Shaun asked.

Kim strolled into the kitchen in time to hear Shaun's question. "My baby isn't around any of those little pouffie mouth tramps."

"Yeah, right!" Shaun said. "CEO of Vespasian, I imagine they're draped all over my man."

"CEO of Vespasian?" Kim laughed. "Sterling, what have you been telling these guys?"

"He hasn't told us a thing," Shaun told her. "His doesn't have to open his mouth, his name speaks for itself."

"You guys have been tasting way too many margarita mixes up in here," Kim said laughing.

David wrapped his arm around Sterling. "You hit the jackpot with this one, Kimmie!"

"One day, you'll be Mrs. Vespasian," Shaun said.

"What on Earth are you two talking about?"

"I'm talking about my man Sterling," David said. "As the CEO's wife, you'll get first dibs on all the latest high dollar stuff."

"Sterling is not the CEO of Vespasian," Kim said, waving them off.

All eyes in the room shifted to Sterling.

"Actually, I am."

Kim recoiled slightly.

"Come on Kimmie, don't pretend like you didn't know!" Shaun said, wrapping his arms around her.

"I didn't," Kim said softly. "*CEO*, Sterling?"

Sterling shrugged.

"Why didn't you tell me?" Kim asked. It was almost a whisper.

"Tell you what?" Sterling asked, turning up his palms. "I thought you knew. I mean, the subject never really came up. You knew that I was an executive, I figured you kinda knew what my position was."

"No, I didn't. How could I have known, unless you told me. *CEO*?" Kim turned to Shaun. "How long have you known."

"David told me," Shaun said pointing toward him.

Kim turned toward David. "How long have you known?"

"Since the library dedication," David said softly.

"Library dedication?" She turned toward Sterling, who lowered his head. She turned back toward David. "What library dedication?"

"At The New York School for The Gifted and Talented," David told her.

"You gave money to a library?" Kim asked Sterling.

Sterling nodded.

"A library? What library?" Kim's thought process worked rapidly. Like all New Yorkers she knew of the Gifted and Talented school. She also knew what grade levels the school taught. Still, she had to ask the question; she had to hear it from him. "Why *that* particular school, Sterling?"

"Because my son goes there."

Kimberly's mouth fell open and she gasped. Her breathing became heavy and labored.

"Kim…" Sterling reached for her.

"No!" She pulled away, and began backing out of the kitchen. "You have a *son*, Sterling?"

"Yes," Sterling said, reaching for her again. "I was going to talk to you about that."

"You were going to talk to me about it?" Kim shouted. "When? When were you going to tell me that you had a child, Sterling? When? At his graduation? When his mother busted out my car windows?"

"It's not like that, Kim."

"It's not like what?" Kim shouted. "You have a child, Sterling! A child!"

"I was going to tell you about him!"

"I asked you, Sterling! I asked you, and you lied to me! I can't believe you lied to me!"

"I didn't lie to you. I never got a chance to tell you."

"You never got a chance to tell me?" Kim shouted. "All of the time that we've spent together, and you couldn't find ten seconds to tell me that you had a child?"

"Kim…"

"No, Sterling! You deceived me! You *lied* to me, and you betrayed my trust in you?"

"How did I betray your trust?"

"I had a *right* to know, Sterling! I should have been able to decide whether I wanted to be in a relationship with you. I should have been able to make that decision, before my heart got involved. I should have been able to make that decision, without getting hurt! What you did, is fucked up, Sterling!"

Brittany and Mia rushed into the kitchen.

"What's going on?" Brittany asked.

"I'm sorry, Brit," Kim told her. "I don't want to ruin your birthday, so I'm going to go."

"Kim, what's the matter?" Mia asked.

"This asshole is the CEO of Vespasian, *and* he has a child!"

Mia and Brittany both shifted their glance toward Sterling.

"I have a son," Sterling announced. "His name is Sterling Barrington Williams III. He is my only child. I was once married, and he is a product of that marriage."

Kim began to hyperventilate. "You don't think I should have known all of this? *You son of a bitch!*"

"Kim…"

Brittany held up her hand, stopping him. Mia grabbed Kim, and led her out of the kitchen and into the bedroom to lay down.

"Brit…"

Brittany again held up her hand and silenced him. "Sterling, I don't know what to say, or what to tell you. But for right now, I think that it's best that you leave. We'll take care of Kimmie. All I can say is that I'll be praying that everything works out for you two, and that she'll call you when she's ready."

Sterling headed for the door, with the crowd parting and making way for him. Passing through the apartment full of judgmental eyes made him feel a way that he had never felt before. He was the CEO of his own company. He had graduated Magna Cum Laude from Harvard. He had graduated at the top of his high school class. Never in his life had he been made to feel inadequate until that moment.

Their eyes made him feel as though he were the lowest life form on Earth, and that he didn't deserve to be among human beings. He closed the door to the apartment, wondering what had went wrong, and how things had degenerated so rapidly. He went from wanting to marry Kim, to being the bane of her existence. How he was going to make this one right, he had no idea. But what he did know, was that he loved her, and that he was *in love* with her. He knew that he wanted to share the rest of his life with her.

Just Another Damn Love Story

Chapter Twenty Three

"Come in!" Sterling shouted.

Gianna pushed open the door to his office and stepped inside. "You wanted to see me, boss?"

"Yes," Sterling waved his hand, motioning for her to take the seat opposite his desk. "Sit down."

Gianna seated herself, and crossed her legs.

"Wilson tells me that you turned down his offer to be CEO of our women's line."

Gianna leaned back in her seat. "I did."

"Why? Gianna, don't you realize the importance of this position? It's a huge jump in pay for you. It would also make you a vice president in the parent company."

"Some things are more important than money," she told him.

This time, it was Sterling who leaned back. He examined her carefully, as if to try to gain some measure of her soul.

"This promotion, it would mean that I would have to leave Italy and come to America. I do not want to leave my family. Italy is my home."

"You can fly home on the weekends if you like."

Gianna shook her head. "No thanks, I'll pass."

"I can't believe you are turning down this promotion."

Gianna shrugged. "What does this promotion give me that I don't already have? Money? I make plenty of money. Freedom? I have complete creative freedom already. It would bring only headache, and distract me from what I truly love, which is design."

Sterling exhaled. He knew that she was right. But he also knew that she would have been perfect for the position. Now, he would have to keep searching. The question was, once he found someone, what if that person's vision clashed with Gianna's? Would he back Gianna, his bread and butter? The woman whose vision had taken his company thus far? Or would he back his new CEO? No doubt he would probably end up backing Gianna, the young woman who had been with him almost from the start. But that would definitely leave bad blood between him and his newly hired executive. And in this industry, where egos were larger than entire solar systems, perceived slights could come back and haunt a person years down the line.

"You're thinking about me?" Gianna asked with a smile. "Taking my measure. Wondering who is this woman who turns down this glorious position?"

Sterling laughed.

"I never wanted my own house," Gianna told him, in her thick Italian accent. "I only wanted to design beautiful clothes."

Sterling nodded. "I remember."

Gianna smiled. It was a crooked little smile, one that only she and the Mona Lisa could conjure. "I was sixteen."

"That day outside of the fashion expose in Milan," Sterling continued.

"And you were the only one who would listen to me," Gianna said. "You took the time to look at a young girls design portfolio. The *only* one."

"I'm glad that I did," Sterling said. "Even then, your designs were ahead of their time. You are an amazing talent."

Gianna nodded. "And you are an amazing person for seeing it, and for giving me a chance. It is he who has the bigger heart, who sees and encourages greatness in others. I remember my grandmother telling me, that the true measure of a person's soul, is how they treat someone who can do nothing for them. I could do nothing for you, Sterling, and yet you treated me with respect, and kindness, and dignity."

Sterling ran his hands over his face, rubbing his weary eyes.

"Long days?" Gianna asked, lifting an eyebrow.

"Even longer nights," Sterling said nodding.

"Love is not worth it, if it doesn't make you suffer."

"What?" He lifted his head. Her statement had taken him by surprise.

"But in the end, you must go to her," Gianna continued. "You must make things right."

"What are you talking about?" Sterling asked. "What have you heard?"

"Everything," Gianna smiled. "This industry is too small to keep secrets. Especially secrets of the heart. The great Sterling Williams and the love of his life had a public falling out? Wilson and Marvette pulled every string they had to keep it out of the tabloids. But still, models talk."

"Ah," Sterling nodded. There had been several models at the party. As well as a few people he recognized from various magazines. He knew that eventually things would get out. He figured that he would probably make page three of the Posts, and maybe even page five of the Times. He was grateful to Wilson and to his publicist that they had been able to squash the story and keep it out of the papers and the tabloids.

"You love her?" Gianna asked.

Sterling nodded, while staring off into space.

"And she is upset because you lied to her?"

"I did not tell her about Third," Sterling explained.

"And this woman, she is angry because of this?" Gianna asked, with her thick Italian accent on full display. "She should have been happy. You have a family already, and she didn't have to lay on the table and let the doctor take it out of her!"

Sterling laughed heartily. "American women don't think like that, Gianna."

"Why not? Woman is woman. No pain is good. American woman have baby *is* pain, Italian woman have baby *is* pain. All the same. No pain is good!"

"She feels like I lied to her," Sterling

explained. "Like I deceived her because I didn't tell her. She had problems with her last boyfriend because of his children's mothers."

"And she blames you for this?"

Sterling shook his head. "No, but she doesn't want to go through the same thing again."

"This I don't understand. They say that America is great. Land of optimism. But yet, people in America are cynical. They don't give chances here in America. This woman, she did not give you chance to fail or succeed."

"She did," Sterling said softly. "And I failed her."

"No," Gianna said, shaking her head. "You are not that man, Sterling Williams. I know you."

"I did, Gianna," Sterling told her. "I should have told her. I could have told her any number of times. I was just so scared that I would mess things up. I kept putting it off. I kept telling myself that I would tell her at the right time. I was always searching for a better time, but that time never came."

"And now her heart is broken because she feels like she cannot trust you?" Gianna asked.

"Exactly," Sterling said, nodding.

"I vouch for you," Gianna smiled. "Sterling is

good man. A man who gives people chances. A man who sees the best in people. I trust, and so she can trust."

"I wish it were that easy."

"I'm flying back to Italy on Friday," Gianna told him. "How is the women's line coming along?"

"Very well," Sterling said, piping up. "We just need someone to run the show for us."

"I have the designs ready for fall, winter, spring, and summer. You will love them all. Also, I have designed two more handbags, and a line of scarves."

"You are *fantastic*, Gianna. I don't know what we would do without you."

"You know that I hired my younger sister."

Sterling nodded. "I heard something about that."

"She is more talented than me," Gianna smiled. "Wait until I send you some of *her* designs."

"I can't wait to see them."

"I will run the line for you from Italy, until you find someone, Sterling."

"Gianna, it really has to be done from here," Sterling told her. "If for no other reason than the daily stuff that we need to consult on. Everything is basically done from here. Our marketing department is here, our finance department is here, our buyer coordinator, our entire corporate structure is here. Italy is basically our faux corporate headquarters and our design studio. There is no way to run a major division of the company outside of this building. You'd be on the telephone or in video conference ninety percent of the day."

"I'll fly back and forth to New York, and help to get the house set up, until you find someone permanently."

"It will take away from your design time," Sterling warned.

"I want to help you, Sterling."

"What changed your mind, Gianna?"

"Remembering how you gave a sixteen year old girl a chance."

"You're the right person for this job," Sterling told her.

"As soon as you find someone, I want out. I go back to my little design studio."

"Little?" Sterling lifted an eyebrow and smiled. "Your little design studio is bigger than my new office. Five times bigger!"

"Oh Sterling, let's not fuss over the little things."

"I guess I can't complain," Sterling smiled.

"You're a vice president now. Vice President of Vespasian Group, and CEO of Vespasian Woman Ltd."

Gianna nodded. "I like the sound of that."

Again Sterling leaned back in his chair. "Well, at least I solved one problem today."

"Sterling, do you want me to kick her ass for you?"

"No thanks, Gianna. I'm not sure you could handle her anyway."

"Don't let my size fool you."

Sterling laughed. "I'm going to call Wilson and tell him the good news."

Gianna rose. "I'll need an office here."

"You already have one. We cleared out an office down the hall for whoever the new VP was going to be."

"Hmmm. Well, I guess I'll go and check out my new office." Gianna turned and headed for the door. She paused and turned back to him after opening it. "Sterling. I'm worried about you."

"Why?"

"Because I don't want you to grow an American heart," she told him. "You can't stop giving chances to others. Even to this woman who won't give you chance. Send her flowers, and don't stop giving her chances. It is good for your heart."

Sterling nodded. "I won't give up, Gianna. And, Gianna…"

"Yes?"

"Thank you for not giving up on me."

Chapter Twenty Four

Kimberly ran her thumb down the seam of her panties, pulling them out of her butt, before flouncing down onto Mia's bed.

"Girl, you still got a booty bite!" Brittany told her.

"That's because she's put on about six pounds in as many days," Mia said.

"You and those Bon Bon ice cream balls ain't no joke," Brittany told Kim, slapping her across her booty.

"Can't you two just let me wallow in my depression in peace?" Kim asked.

"Don't think so." Brittany said.

"Why are you depressed again?" Mia asked.

"Don't be funny," Kim said rolling her eyes. "Your man is down in the polls by two percentage points."

"Okay, you didn't have to go there!" Mia said,

standing up. "Those polls don't mean a thing! They were expected to get a bounce after their little lying convention! Don't you take your little hysterics out on my candidate. Just because you and your little boyfriend are having problems, you don't have to go there!"

Mia lifted her stuffed Barack Obama doll and hugged it and kissed it. "Don't you listen to her, my little baby Barack. We are going to win re-election, and we are going to stay inside of that big old White House. Yes we are, my little pookey, because *yes we can!*"

"You need some mental help," Kim told her.

"Both of you are crazy," Brittany told them.

"She's the one that's crazy," Mia said. "Girl, so what, your man is a CEO of a major company? What, you want to break up with him because he can afford to buy the island instead of just vacation on it? Girl, you are tripping!"

"Tripping?" Kim asked, peering up at Mia. "See, no more BET for you. You and those damn music videos…"

Brittany burst into laughter. "Okay?"

"And for your information, it's more than just the fact that he has money," Kim continued. "I knew that he had money, it's the principal of the matter. He should have told me who he was."

"Didn't he introduce himself as Sterling Williams?" Mia asked.

"Yes."

"It's not his fault that his name didn't register," Mia told her.

"Mia, I showed this man my *designs*!" Kim said.

"Oh, so *that's* it!" Brittany shouted. "This is really all about Kimberly! Someone is embarrassed about opening up to someone else. She feels exposed. She showed her design sketches to someone in the industry. Someone who could help her, by the way, and so she feels exposed."

"I knew the truth would come out," Mia said, staring at Brittany.

"Don't you guys even care that he deceived me?" Kim fired back. "This man has an entire family out there, that he didn't bother to tell me about. Don't you think that I should have been told?"

"Okay, I agree with you on that one," Brittany told her. "He should have told you about his son."

"He's divorced, Kim," Mia said. "He doesn't have an entire family out there, he just has a son.

Granted, he should have told you about his son. But, think about it like this, would you have given the relationship a chance had you known about his son?"

"No, but that's my *choice*!" Kim told her. "I have a right to make that choice!"

"You think that you get to choose your life's direction?" Brittany asked with a smile. "You think that you have a choice who you fall in love with?"

Kim nodded. "Yes. We all have a choice. We can make good decisions with our life, or we can make bad ones. I chose to go to Princeton. You two *chose* to go to Princeton. We could have all skipped college, and went to work at McDonald's. But we didn't. We chose to make a good decision and go to an Ivy League school. Life is about the choices we make. And I'll be damned if I let someone take away my *choices*!"

"No one has to take away your choices, Kimmie," Brittany told her. "You've taken them all away on your own! You've put blinders on, and you've narrowed the path that you have to walk in life so much that you can't see the wonderful things that blindside you sometimes. Don't be afraid of getting blindsided by happiness. That's how God sends some of the most wonderful things our way."

"It never happens by design, or when we plan it to," Mia added. "Remember the saying? You want to see God laugh, make a plan. You remember that, Kimmie?"

"Sterling came out of nowhere, and he struck like a thunderstorm," Brittany continued. "He hit hard, and fast, and furious. He took you out of your doldrums, and he showed you that it was okay to love again."

"We hadn't seen you that happy in a long time," Mia told her.

"But you know what, Kimme?" Brittany asked.

"What?" Kim asked softly.

"As much as he showed you that it was okay to love again, you have to convince yourself that it's okay to trust again," Brittany said. "No one can give you permission to do that. That's something that your heart has to do for itself."

"How can I trust a man who didn't tell me that he had a kid?" Kim asked.

"That's an answer that you have to find for yourself, kid," Brittany told her. "But I do know, that that man loves you."

"How do you know that?"

"Because I got a damn living room full of

roses that he's been sending here for the last three days!" Mia said. "Bitch, if he sends anymore, I'm kicking you and your flowers out!"

The three of them burst into laughter.

"Why would he hesitate to tell you about someone so important in his life?" Brittany said. "David said that he absolutely adores his son. That he gave tens of millions of dollars to a school, and donated a library in his son's name. Now, why would someone who loves their child so much, hesitate to tell you about him?"

Kimberly rolled over on her back and stared at Brittany.

"Because he loves you just as much, and was afraid of losing you," Brittany told her. "How can you run away from a man who loves you that much?"

Kimberly punched the bed with her fists. "Just let me be angry, you two!"

The doorbell rang, and Mia rushed to her door and opened it. It was a delivery man with more flowers.

Mia signed for the flowers, and then turned toward Kim. "Bitch get out!"

Again they laughed.

"Get some Claritin and leave me alone," Kim

told Mia, before rolling over onto her stomach again.

"You're not sleeping in my bed again tonight, Kim," Mia told her.

"Why not?"

"Because, last night, I thought I felt you rubbing on my titties."

"Uuuuughhhh, you two are nasty!" Brittany said laughing.

"Bitch, please!" Kim shouted. "You don't even have any titties!"

Mia lifted her shirt and began dancing around the apartment.

"I know what we need," Brittany told them. "We need to hit the club."

Kimberly shook her head. "No, I know what I need to do."

"What's that?" Mia asked.

"I need to go home to my Mommy and Daddy," Kim told them.

"Are you sure you're ready to deal with your mom right now?" Mia asked.

Kim shook her head. "Of course not. But I need to curl up in my old bed, surrounded by all of my stuffed animals, and think about my life."

"You want me to go with you?" Mia asked,

rubbing Kim's back.

"No, I can handle it. I just want to go home. To that familiar place where I can walk around, feel safe, and think."

"I understand," Brittany said, nodding. "But I do have a question."

"What's that?" Kim asked.

"I thought your Porsche was in the shop?" Brittany asked. "How are you going to get there?"

"It is," Kim said with a smile. "But your Benz isn't."

"My new Benz?" Brittany asked.

Kim held out her hands for the keys. Brittany went into her purse and tossed Kimberly her keys.

"My new Mercedes SLS AMG Black Label convertible," Brittany whimpered. "Be careful with my baby."

"Westchester County in a car that goes two hundred miles per hour?" Kimberly smiled. "I'll be there and out of the car in a flash."

Brittany shook her head. "Don't play with me."

"I'll be back Sunday night, Monday at the latest." Kim said, rising from Mia's bed. She grabbed an outfit from Mia's closet and tossed it onto the bed.

"Hey, that's my Dolce & Gabbana!" Mia shouted.

"Are you going to deprive a depressed woman?" Kim asked, slipping into the outfit.

"If anything happens to that outfit, depression will be the *least* of your worries!" Mia told her.

Kimberly opened her arms wide, and Mia and Brittany joined her for a group hug.

"I love you guys," Kim told them.

"We love you too!" Brittany and Mia said in unison.

"Brit, while I'm gone, get Mia some help," Kim said.

"Why?"

"She sleeps in the bed with that little Chucky looking Barack Obama doll," Kim told her.

"You two bitches are the weirdest sisters a girl could ask for," Brittany said laughing.

"Kim, don't go there with my little Barack!" Mia told her. "I'll get all Lucy Lu on your ass about my Little Barack baby."

Again, the three of them hugged tightly.

Just Another Damn Love Story

Chapter Twenty Five

Marjorie Neel pulled her baking sheet out of the oven and placed in on top of her stainless steel stove. She lifted a spatula, and lifted two piping hot cookies off of the sheet and placed them inside of a bowl. She then walked to her freezer, pulled out a half gallon of vanilla ice cream, and took it back to the counter with her, where she scooped some of the ice cream into the bowl with the hot cookies. Afterward, she carried her bowl of cookies and ice cream to the bar and presented it to Kimberly.

"Mommy's little buttercup's favorite!" she said, placing the bowl down in front of Kimberly. "You eat up. Dinner will be ready in a little while. Mommy is making her baby's favorite! Lobster and shrimp, with garlic butter noodles on the side."

Kimberly rolled her eyes.

"So, when are we going to meet that wonderful boyfriend of yours?" Marjorie asked.

"Oh, so now he's a *wonderful* boyfriend?" Kim asked, rolling her eyes toward the ceiling again. Her mother had been treating her like she was Queen Elizabeth since she pulled into the driveway. It was even worse than her constant berating. At least she could say that her mother was only nagging because she cared, but this hypocrisy was a horse of an entirely different color.

"Yes, he's always been a *wonderful* man in my eyes," Marjorie gushed. "And your father and I can't wait to meet him!"

"And this has nothing to do with the fact that he's the CEO and majority owner of Vespasian?" Kim asked. "And it has nothing to do with the fact that he's famous, and fabulously wealthy?"

Marjorie waved her hand dismissing her daughter's statements. "Oh, of course not. But it doesn't hurt that my future son-in-law is rich and famous either!"

"*Future son-in-law?*" Kimberly recoiled. "Mother! Last week he wasn't good enough to mow your lawn! Now he's your *future son-in-law?*"

"Oh, Kimberly, don't be so overly sensitive!" Marjorie told her. "You always were a sensitive child. Don't take everything so literally."

"Literally? You were in love with John last

week. At least until you found out that Sterling was super rich!"

"What do I care about how rich he is?" Marjorie asked, placing her hand against her chest. "It's all about how well he treats you, my dear."

"And it isn't about the fact that he's wealthier than Mrs. Witherspoon's son-in-law, who happened to be the richest son-in-law of all the members of your little bridge club?"

Marjorie's wide grin was uncontrollable. "It's not about that old bat! Even though I can't wait to see the look on her face Thursday night! This is about you, sweetie."

"And it's not about being able to brag about him in the church choir, or about throwing his name around at your next little Links meeting, or your Girlfriends Club, or at your little country club?"

Again, Marjorie waved off her daughter's comments. "What kind of pariah do you think I am? Is that the kind of person you think I am? A social climber who just wants to name drop? Is that who you believe I am?"

"I believe that you're a mother who is overly competitive, just like the rest of your friends."

"Kimberly, stop it."

"So, it wouldn't bother you if I told you that

Sterling and I were no longer together?"

"Child have you bumped your head?" Marjorie shouted.

Kimberly smiled. "I knew it!"

"What do you mean, no longer together?" Marjorie asked. "You are just testing me, aren't you?"

"Sterling and I broke up."

"Are you crazy?" Marjorie snapped. "What ever for?"

"He lied to me," Kimberly explained. "He deceived me."

"Deceived you how?"

"He has a son, Mother. A son from a previous marriage that he didn't tell me about."

"And that's why you broke up with him? Because he has a child from a previous marriage? Kimberly, are you on drugs?"

"He should have told me about him!"

"Kimberly, men are not perfect," Marjorie said, seating herself on the stool next to her daughter. "I'm sorry to tell you this. I guess your father and I sheltered you and your sister, and we built up this little fairy tale world for you, but the truth of the matter is, no one is perfect. Even your father has flaws that I have to put up with."

"Like what?"

"Like his snoring!" Beverly said, shouting into the family so that she could be heard. "And his stinky socks!"

"That's not the same, Mother."

"It is the same," Marjorie told her. "You can't run around this world thinking that everything and everyone should be the way you want them to be. You're looking for perfect in an imperfect world."

"You thought that John was perfect."

"Marjorie waved her hand dismissing the statement. "Ah, who cares about that loser!"

"Mother! You thought the world of him last week!"

"Forget about the past, dear!" Marjorie told her daughter. "Look to the future. Let us look to our Sterling. So what, he has a child from a previous marriage. As long as he is a responsible man, and as long as he does the right thing for the child, then there is nothing to worry about. And from what I hear, he loves that boy. In fact, he loves him enough to dedicate a multi-million dollar learning center in his name. Sterling is a winner, dear!"

"Mother, being rich doesn't mean that he's a winner!" Kimberly protested. She shook her head and exhaled. "I'm not ready to play step mom."

"You played step mother with John's brood," Marjorie reminded her.

"I don't want to go through this whole baby momma drama thing again!" Kim told her.

"And who says that you will?" Marjorie asked.

Kim shook her head and rose. "This is not my life! This is not how I pictured my life to be! Everyone is running my life, manipulating things, making decisions for me! *I* control me! I'm taking my life back."

"Oh, Kimberly!" Marjorie said. "Stop being so melodramatic!"

"Heads up!"

Kim turned in the directions from which the voice came. It was her father.

"Catch!" Thornton told her. He tossed her an old, well worn, catcher's mitt.

"Dad!" Kimberly shouted, catching the mitt.

"*Thornton*!" Marjorie shouted. "How many times do I have to remind you that we have young ladies? They're not little girls anymore, and we didn't have a son."

Thornton smiled, as he bounced a baseball up and down in the palm of his hand. "How about a game of catch, Kimmie? For old time's sake?"

Marjorie leaned in toward Kimberly. "I don't think your father ever got over not having a son."

"*Poppycock!*" Thornton told her. "I have two daughters, and I've never been happier or prouder."

Kim smiled, and headed out of the front door and into the front yard with her father. Thornton walked to one side of the yard, while Kimberly took up a position on the other side. Thornton tossed Kimberly the ball, and she caught it.

"Thanks for rescuing me," Kimberly told him.

"We all need a little rescuing sometimes," Thornton smiled.

Kimberly threw the ball back, and Thornton caught it.

"I see you still have that great arm," Thornton told her.

"Dad! My arm never was that great. You just made me feel like it was. You always had a habit of that."

"Of what?"

"Of making me feel like I was really special," Kimberly told him. "Maybe that's why my standards are so high. I'm looking for a guy who'll make me feel as great as you made me feel."

Thornton smiled. "Any luck?"

Kimberly shrugged. "Sterling had a habit of doing the same thing. Always encouraging me, and making me think that I was better at something than I really was, or making me think that I can do anything."

Thornton lifted an eyebrow. "Oh really?"

He threw the ball back to Kimberly and she caught it.

"Yeah. He was always telling me that I can eventually start my own clothing line, or design for a major company. He was always challenging me to believe in myself and my abilities."

"Sounds like a great guy," Thornton told her.

"He was in some ways," Kim admitted. "And in other ways, he turned out to be nothing more than a great big liar."

"Oh, well, we don't need to talk about him then," Thornton told her.

"Good!" Kimberly huffed. She threw the ball back to her father.

"I saw a really great show the other night on the Discovery Channel," Thornton said, catching the ball. He threw it back.

"Oh, yeah?" Kim said, catching the ball. "What was it about?"

"It was about the books of the Bible,"

Thornton told her. "Can you believe that Mary Magdalene wrote a Gospel?"

"I read about that in USA Today once."

"Can you believe that Judas Iscariot wrote a Gospel?"

"Get out of here!" Kimberly said. "What would he have to write about?"

"Well, it turns out, according to this gospel, The Gospel of Judas, that Jesus went to Judas, and told him that he was going to turn him in to the Romans. In fact, the gospel says, Judas didn't betray Jesus, he turned Him in because Jesus asked Judas to. Can you believe that?"

Kimberly shook her head. "That's crazy!"

"Yeah!" Thornton said nodding. "Jesus gave Judas a commission, and Judas carried it out. Crazy how life works, isn't it? And up until this gospel was found, we all vilified Judas as the ultimate traitor. But now, scholars are re-examining his role. If this gospel is true, then Judas sacrificed his good name for all eternity, to carry out God's instructions."

"Wow," Kim lowered her glove and walked to the same side of the yard where her father was standing. "You should have recorded the show for me."

"It'll come back on," Thornton told her. "And I'll record it then. We can sit down with a bowl of popcorn and watch it together. It'll be like old times. You and me, and a giant bowl of popcorn in front of the TV."

"I look forward to that," Kimberly told her father.

"That is an amazing story," Thornton continued. "Just goes to show us, we don't always understand God's plans for us, but we just have to be ready to embrace the challenges that He places in front of us."

Kimberly nodded.

"I didn't raise my daughters to run away at the first sign of trouble," Thornton continued. "So I know, when God places some new or difficult challenge in front of them, they'll step up to the plate. Running away from challenges, is running away from God's potential rewards and blessings."

Kimberly exhaled and rested her head on her father's chest.

"Forgiveness, Kimmie, is a wonderful virtue," Thornton said, caressing her head. "When we forgive others, it gives us permission to go on with our lives and find our own happiness."

"How can you trust someone who deceived

you twice?"

"It doesn't matter what he does for a living. Perhaps he didn't tell you about that because he's been hurt by women only wanting to date him for his money? But I really don't even think that the fault lies with him on that issue, Kimmie, because he did tell you his real name, didn't he?"

Kimberly nodded.

"Did you ever say anything to him about not wanting to date a man with kids?" Thornton asked. "Did you happen to mention what you went through with John and his kids and their mothers?"

Again, Kimberly nodded.

"Was this after you two had fallen for one another?"

Kimberly nodded.

"So, feelings were already involved, and he was scared that you would cut him off completely once you found out."

Kim nodded.

"Which you did, once you found out."

"Oh, Daddy!" Kimberly said, wrapping her arms around her father. "I'm so confused about this whole thing."

"I can't give you the answers that you seek, Kimmie," Thornton told her. "This is your life, and you have to make the right decision for you. I'm here to listen, and to give you fatherly advice, but in the end, you have to make the final decision because you have to live with it. But no matter what you decide, just remember this; it takes a lot more energy to be angry with someone, than it does to just forgive and move on. Don't carry around that kind of baggage, Kimmie. Anger, or hatred, or bitterness, it's all corrosive. Don't keep that inside of you."

Kimberly nodded. "I won't, Daddy. I love you."

"I love you too, sweetheart."

Chapter Twenty Six

Wilson strolled into Sterling's office. "Time to snap out of it."

"Snap out of what?" Sterling asked.

"Everyone says that you've been moping around here lately and acting like a real asshole."

"Really?" Sterling asked, lifting an eyebrow.

"Yeah. I've seen the moping, but I can't tell if you've been acting like an asshole, because to me, you've always acted like an ass."

"Real funny."

"See, you used to laugh when I insult you."

"Sorry."

"Sterling, call her."

"I tried that for three weeks, remember? She doesn't want to talk to me."

"So, you're just going to give up?" Wilson asked. "The Sterling that I know isn't a quitter. And if you've become one, then we all may as well pack up and leave. This is too tough a business for quitters."

"Anyone feel like I've been too harsh on them lately, I'll gladly accept their resignation," Sterling told him. "Pass the word."

"I got a better idea. How about you stop being a dick, and start being the Sterling that everyone knows and loves? How about we go out, hit the town, find some honeys, and then hit Atlantic City for the weekend? How about I hook you up with a real cutie pie, so that you can start the process of picking up the pieces and moving on? If you've really given up on Kimberly, that is?"

Sterling exhaled, and slid a brochure across his desk for Wilson to look at. "The new Gulfstream business jet."

Wilson lifted the brochure and flipped through a few pages. "Nice. Have you called them already?"

Sterling nodded.

"So you're serious this time, about getting a private jet?"

Again Sterling nodded.

"What does one of these set you back for nowadays?" Wilson asked.

"About forty million," Sterling told him. "At

least in the configuration that I want."

Wilson whistled. "That's a lot of pennies out of the piggy bank."

"I need it."

"You don't need it, you *want* it," Wilson corrected him. "It's more convenient for you. But at the end of the day, when the FAA says that planes aren't flying because of the weather, your ass is still going to be stuck like everyone else."

"Yeah, but how often is that going to happen? I'm going to enjoy the convenience of flying out whenever I need to, and not having to go through those ridiculous airport lines and screeners. I won't have to deal with baggage claim, or lost luggage, or be subject to the airlines latest whim."

Wilson nodded. "Expensive habit. I'd rather pick up something cheaper, like top notch Cuban cigars or something."

Sterling cracked a smile.

"Holy miracle!" Wilson shouted, pointing toward Sterling. "I can't believe that the vampire actually smiled."

"How's the executive search going?" Sterling asked.

"Slow. But Gianna is doing a stand up job."

"Of course," Sterling nodded. "We both knew

that she would. But that doesn't stop her from emailing me everyday asking about her replacement."

"Too bad."

"Too bad what?"

"Kim would have been perfect for the position," Wilson suggested. "She has a business degree. She's in the industry. She's also a talented designer. She vibes with the company really well. She would have been perfect for the position."

Sterling leaned back in his chair. "You love torturing me, don't you?"

Wilson shook his head. "I'm not torturing you. You're torturing you. Pick up the phone, and call that women. If that doesn't work, grab your keys, and go and stand outside of her apartment."

"Oh, *yeah right*! You can really see me doing that?"

"Why not? Because you're the great Sterling Williams? Pride will make you lose the one you love if you're not careful."

Sterling slid Wilson another brochure. "This is the new Bombadier jet."

"That's one's nice too."

"And this is one from Dassault, and this one's from Embraer."

Wilson lifted the brochures and began to flip through them.

"I'm thinking about grabbing a plane for the company to use, in addition to my personal one."

"Now you're talking!" Wilson said, taking a seat. "I could get used to flying in one of these."

"A minute ago you thought it was a waist of money."

"That was before I knew that I would be relaxing my ass on some of this fine Italian leather."

Sterling threw his head back in laughter. It was the first good laugh he'd had in weeks.

*****

Laquisha stormed into Kimberly's office. "Finally, you decided to come to work!"

"Laquisha, you know that I've been going through some things," Kimberly told her. She sniffled, and pulled some tissue from a nearby Kleenex box and wiped her nose.

"Your personal problems, have nothing to do with me or with this company!" Laquisha told her. "If you having boyfriend problems, you take care of that shit on your personal time!"

"Laquisha, I took some personal days off, because I had accrued that time. I took sick leave off Monday and Tuesday, because I was sick, and I had sick leave days that I hadn't used yet."

"When I made you a manager, I didn't know that you would stop working, and start loafing and taking days off!"

"Start loafing? I haven't been loafing! I had sick leave, so I took it? Why is that a problem?"

"It's a problem because I need people who are going to be here!" Laquisha shouted. "It's a problem, because you haven't brought in any new clients in three weeks! It's a problem, because you stopped producing once you got promoted. And so now, my only option is to put someone in this position who can do the job!"

Kimberly rose from her desk. "Laquisha, no!"

"I need someone who can bring in clients, and manage this department and the other advertising executives and reps."

"Laquisha I'm here!" Kim pleaded. "I was going through some things, but I'm back on the ball now. Just give me a couple of days to pull in some revenue."

"You bring in some revenue in the next couple

of days, and you can keep your job as an ad exec. You don't, and you're out of here. But you're no longer a department manager."

Kimberly fell back into her seat. "Laquisha, I can't."

"Can't what?"

"I can't walk out of this office and face them," Kim said. "I can't pack up my things and move back into the room with everyone else, and have to look at the smirks, and listen to the whispers and the snickers. I can't go out there as a failure."

"Do what you have to do."

"Do what I have to do?" Kim said forcefully. "Is that all you have to say to me, after I've given you years of service, and brought in millions of dollars in ad revenue for this magazine? Do what I have to do? Is that what all of my years of dedication and hard work boil down to? Is that how this is going to end?"

"If that's how you choose to end it." Laquisha said coldly.

Kimberly rose from her desk. "You bitch! You pudgy, big lip, bell pepper nosed bitch! I can't believe you!"

"Get out!" Laquisha shouted, pointing toward the door.

"You're god damned right I'm getting out!" Kimberly told her. She began gathering her personal belongings.

"Get out now!" Laquisha shouted. "Your shit will be mailed to you. You get the fuck out of this building right now!"

"I'll leave once I've gathered my belongings!" Kimberly shouted.

"You'll leave now, before I call security!" Laquisha said, lifting the telephone.

Kimberly snatched the receiver out of Laquisha's hand, and slammed the telephone back down onto its base. "Don't make me put you to the test, Laquisha!"

"What?" Laquisha recoiled.

"I said, don't make me pull your card, and see how much you're really from the streets, as you like to claim you are."

"I'm a professional!" Laquisha shouted. "You can just get out of this office, and out of this building."

Kimberly continued to gather her belongings. "I'll leave, once I've finished collecting my things."

Laquisha folded her arms and shifted her weight to one side.

Kimberly pulled a drawer completely out of

her desk, and began to pile her belongings inside of it.

"That drawer belongs to the company!" Laquisha told her.

"I'll bring it back to the company, as soon as I've place my belongings in my car!" Kim told her.

"What's going on?" Pamela asked, rushing into the office. "I can hear you two shouting all the way down the hall!"

"I quit!" Kimberly told her.

"No, you're fired!" Laquisha shouted.

"No, *bitch*, I *quit!*" Kimberly said, lifting the drawer with her belongings, and heading for the door."

Pamela clapped her hands. "Good for you, girl!"

"Bitch, you can go with her!" Laquisha shouted.

"You know what, Laquisha?" Pamela said. "I think I will. I quit too, you fat bitch!"

"You can take this job, and stick it up the deepest darkest part of your stinky ass!" Kim shouted.

Kimberly and Pamela stepped out of the former's office, and was greeted with applause. They strutted down the hall to the whistles, clapping, and cheers of their former co-workers.

"What are you going to do?" Pamela asked Kimberly, once they reached the elevator.

Kimberly shrugged. "I don't know. And you know what, it feels good not knowing, and even better not giving a shit."

Pamela hi-fived her.

"How about you?" Kim asked. "Are you going to be okay?"

Pamela nodded. "Girl, I got a job at *Essence* on Monday. I was supposed to put in my two weeks notice here today, but…"

Kimberly hugged her. "That's good! Congratulations!"

"Thank you!" Pamela told her. "Are you sure you're going to be alright?"

Kimberly peered around the hall for a few seconds, and then nodded. "I'm going to be all right. In fact, I'm going to be better than I have been in a long time. Girl, it's time for me to do me."

"Right on then, sister!" Pamela said, opening her arms wide.

Kimberly leaned in, and the two of them embraced.

Chapter Twenty Seven

Sterling seated himself on the park bench as he continued to watch Third play. He had his laptop with him, but he didn't feel like opening it up just yet. His son had his full attention for the moment.

That Third was growing and growing fast was obvious to all. Growth was a part of life, but he never thought about that growth as it pertained to his child, or to his life in relation to his child's. He was getting older, and wiser he had hoped. It was that thought that made him wonder what kind of father he was, and what kind of lessons would he be able to instill in his son.

Sterling watched Third's interaction with the other children. He was proud of what he saw thus far. His son had taken turns, broke up an argument between two other children, and had all of the children on the jungle gym playing together. In those few minutes of watching his son he learned that Third was a leader, not a follower. That he was honest, and just, and fair. That he could organize, and that he had a bountiful imagination and a kind heart. Like all fathers, he had hoped and dreamed that his son had taken only the best elements from him. Because like all fathers, his son also carried his hopes and dreams that he would be a better man than he. Third could do more, go further, dream bigger. If he studied hard and got his lesson, he could go to Harvard, and then Harvard Law, and he could be the first Williams to be President of the United States. The world was open to him in ways that had been closed to Sterling. He would do all in his power to make sure that the doors opened wide for his son. He would build an empire, and make sure that his son had the money to make power moves on a global level.

"He's getting bigger and bigger with each passing day."

She had startled him. Sterling quickly turned in the direction from which the voice had came. It was his ex-wife.

"May I?" Carmela asked, waving her hand toward the empty seat next to him on the bench.

"Please," Sterling said, nodding toward the seat.

Carmela seated herself. "He's grown an entire shoe size over the summer."

Sterling smiled and nodded. "I know. I had to buy the new Jordan XX's remember?"

"Oh, that's right," Carmela smiled. "I forgot about that. He's into clothes and how he looks now."

"Must have discovered girls."

"He's like his father," Carmela said smiling. "That boy discovered the opposite sex a long time ago. He's a ham, and a showoff. He can't pass a mirror without checking his waves, or a see a little girl without trying to dance."

Sterling laughed heartily.

"Chile, let me tell you!" Carmela continued. "Have you heard his sexy voice?"

"His sexy voice?"

"Yes! He'll get on the telephone with these little girls, and start talking all slow, and slick."

"Third? Talking to girls on the telephone?"

Carmela nodded. "You're getting old, Sterling. Face it."

"I'm not getting old," Sterling said shaking his head. "I'm getting better."

"We're *both* getting old," Carmela told him.

"Older, but not old."

Carmela hesitated for a few seconds, and then nodded. "Okay, I'll agree with you on that one. Older, but not old."

Sterling peered around the park. "Where did the time go, Carmela?"

"It just went."

"Yeah, but it seems like only yesterday we were both freshmen at Harvard, walking around the yard looking like a pair of deer in some headlights."

"No, sweetie, you looked like a deer caught in some headlights," she corrected him. "That's why I decided to talk to you. I was totally together, so I decided to have some sympathy for the nerdy looking guy."

"Nerdy looking? Woman, I've never looked nerdy in my life!"

"Oh, Sterling, come on! You had a pocket protector!"

"What's nerdy about that? I didn't want my pens to leak into my shirt pocket! Besides, it was a gift from my Nanna."

Carmela shook her head laughing. "What am I going to do with you?"

Sterling shrugged.

"Speaking of Nanna, how is she doing?"

"She's doing well. She asks about you all the

time."

"Give her my love."

"You know, Carmela, you can always go and see them anytime you like. They love you, and they still consider you family. In fact, they are your family too, and always will be."

Carmela shook her head. "Wouldn't feel right."

"With us not being together?"

Carmela nodded slowly.

Sterling leaned back on the bench. "What the hell happened to us, Mel? Were we so damned young, so full of fire, and righteousness, and so egotistical, and hard headed that we couldn't have made it work no matter what?"

Carmela nodded. "Everything became a test of wills between us. A daily battle for supremacy."

Sterling shook his head and peered off into the distance. "The scars."

"The reward," Carmela said softly, nodding toward Third.

Sterling nodded. "The reward."

"He's so much like you, Sterling, that it's not funny."

"I can't get over him trying to talk to girls on the telephone."

"Yep. Next thing you know, it'll be dances and the movies, and then prom, and then off to college, and then a wedding, and one day we'll wake up grandparents."

"Grandparents," Sterling said, exhaling. "I can't even think that far ahead."

"You need to, Sterling," Carmela said softly. "You really should start thinking about what comes next in your life."

"What do you mean?"

"I heard that you had a really nice friend," Carmela explained. "And I also heard that you two broke up, and that you've been miserable ever since."

"Do you know why we broke up?"

"One thing I've learned, is that no matter how thin you slice it, there are always two sides to every story," Carmela told him. "She had some issues with her previous man, about all his baby mommas and their drama. And when she found out about Third, she panicked."

"And you're not upset that I didn't tell her about our son?" Sterling asked.

Carmela shrugged. "Apparently you had your reasons."

Sterling nodded. "I was going to tell her. I

was just waiting for the right opportunity."

"No one's judging you, Sterling. Least of all, me. I know that you're a good father, and I know that you're not ashamed of Third, or of having a son. I knew that you would have told her, because any woman you're with, would have to love him as much as you love him, in order for you to truly love her."

Sterling nodded once again. "Thank you, Mel. You really do understand me."

"You mean, *still* understand you?" she asked, lifting an eyebrow.

"That's right. No one understood me like you did."

Carmela turned back toward the playground. "So, what are you going to do about her?"

Sterling shrugged. "There's nothing that I can do about her."

"You can fight for her."

"Why does that feel so uncomfortable coming from you?" Sterling asked.

"I'm not saying that you should have or that you didn't fight for what we had, Sterling. Our situation was different. We were young, and dumb, and both pissing fire. Neither of us understood what communication meant, or what giving meant, or what it took to sustain a marriage."

"And now that we're older?"

"We have a beautiful son to raise together."

"And that's it?"

"A friendship, Sterling. I want a friendship with you."

"Is that why you're being so nice to me, today?"

"Because you're wounded?" Carmela nodded and smiled. "I don't like to see you wounded, Sterling. Especially if I wasn't the one who shot the arrow."

Sterling laughed heartily. "I can always count on you to keep it real, can't I?"

Carmela nodded. "You bet your ass. That's kinda all I have left in this world. My realness."

"You have a lot more than that."

She shook her head. "Stop with the compliments. I don't want to end up in the sack with you."

"Wouldn't be a bad thing."

"Yes, it would. I don't do rebounds, and I never look back." Carmela paused for several moments. "My question is... do you love her?"

Sterling peered off into the distance for several moments before giving his answer. "I do. I really do."

"Despite your attempt at some sympathy poonanny, I believe that you do." Carmela turned toward Sterling, adjusting herself on the hard wooden bench. "Then go after her, and tell her that you love her. If you're hurting, I'll bet you a dollar to a dime that she's hurting too."

"My question is… can it stay like this between us?" Sterling asked. "Not just while I'm hurting, and while you're feeling sorry for me, but all of the time? I like us like this. I like you being here for me, and being my friend. That is one of the things I miss most, Mel; your friendship."

Carmela nodded. "I'm your friend, Sterling. I have no more anger in my heart toward you. I don't think that I ever really did. I knew how ex wives behaved toward their spouses, and so I figured I was supposed to behave that way. I'm tired of playing the bitter ex spouse. You take really good care of our son, and I have nothing to complain about."

"You should allow me to take care of you also," Sterling told her. "Let me give you a little money each month to help out."

"I'm fine, Sterling. I'm a New York corporate attorney with a degree from Harvard Law, and a business degree from Wharton. I bill my clients out the ass. Besides, if I ever want your money, I'll take you to court, whip your attorney's ass, and bleed you dry."

Again Sterling laughed. He loved Carmela for precisely the reasons she named. She had always been smart, confident, and strong. His love for strong women was something he inherited from watching his mother and his nana work and raise families. They were powerful women, and so was Carmela. He knew it the moment he met her on the yard in Cambridge. He hoped that his son would get lucky and marry a woman like his mother.

"I'm still looking for someone to run the women's line at Vespasian, interested?"

Carmela shook her head. "Not a snowball's chance in hell."

Sterling laughed.

"I hear that the new love of your life is a pretty talented designer, and that she's already in the industry."

Sterling lifted an eyebrow. "You've been talking to Wilson, haven't you?"

"You know that I cannot *stand* Wilson," Carmela said dryly.

"Who's been filling you in?"

"I could tell you, but then I'd have to kill you,"

Carmela said with a smile. "You know I can't reveal my sources."

"Your source has a pretty big mouth."

"That's the way sources usually are. So, are you going to make nice with her or what?"

Sterling shrugged. "What was that you said about not looking back?"

"Touche," she said with a smile. "You got me on that one. But then again, I don't think that this girl is looking back. I think that she's about moving forward. Not often that we professional negroes find someone in our age, income, and education brackets."

"Is that why you're rooting for her?" Sterling asked with a smile.

"Who says that I'm rooting for *her*?" She said, leaning over and nudging his shoulder with hers. "I'm in the Sterling Williams cheering section. I just want you to be happy, babe."

Sterling nodded. "I'm happy."

Carmela rose. "I'll tell you what. You hang out here with him, and I'll go home and cook us all some dinner. You come by, have dinner with us, help him with his homework, and help him get his things together for school tomorrow."

Sterling closed his eyes and shook his head.

"Thank you so much, Mel."

"Don't mention it. Besides, you look like you could use a good meal anyway."

Carmela turned, and strutted away with her Manolo Blahnik heels clicking, leaving him wafting in her Chanel No. 5 perfume.

Chapter Twenty Eight

Kimberly lifted her feet onto the bed, and brushed on another coat of nail polish.

"That color is so pretty!" Mia told her.

"I can't wear that color, and I hate you for being able to!" Brittany told her.

"Why can't you?"

"Because, orange, or peach, or pink just makes me look like a pale, bleached Barbie!" Brittany whined. "I have never been able to wear those colors. I would die to be able to die my hair orange or red."

"Why?" Mia asked, staring at Brittany as if she were crazy. "You have the most beautiful blonde hair in the world. Chicks would die to have your hair."

"And pay good money for it," Kim added. "Blonde is in."

"Is not!" Brittany told them.

"Is too!" Mia said.

"I saw Mary J. at Carnegie during the Wyclef charity show." Brittany told them. "That orange with the blonde tips that she was rocking in that pixie cut, was off the charts!"

"Chain, Brittany," Mia corrected her. "Off the chain."

"Charts, Mia. You say chain, I say charts. How about that?" Brittany leaned forward, and applied a liberal coat of red to her toenails.

Mia began to place tiny diamond studs on her freshly painted toenails in a funky design pattern.

"That is so cute!" Kim told her.

"Thank you," Mia smiled. "You want me to hook you up when I'm done?"

"Do you have enough diamonds?" Kim asked.

Mia lifted a tiny plastic container sitting next to her and shook it. It rattled. "Girl, I got a whole box full."

"I want some!" Brittany said excitedly. She leaped from the couch and raced to where Mia was seated on the floor and plopped down next to her. "Girl, that is so pretty! You need to open up your own shop!"

"Bitch, that is so racist!" Mia shouted.

"What?" Brittany asked, turning up her palms

and staring at Kim.

"I'm Asian, so I need to open up a *nail shop*?" Mia asked.

"I wasn't saying it because you were Asian, but because you're were good at it," Brittany explained.

"And maybe I should talk like this," Mia said in a thick Asian accent. "Ahhh me so horny! Me love you long time!"

Kim and Mia burst into laughter.

"What?" Brittany asked, staring at them with a lost look on her face.

"Relax, bitch!" Mia shouted. "Stop being so sensitive. We don't wear that shit on our shoulder around here!"

Brittany joined in the laughter. "Okay, you got me."

"Besides, if there is any one of us who needs their own business, it's Kimmie here," Mia told them.

"Me?"

Mia nodded. "I saw your new sketches on the table. Girl, I would rock those new peasant blouses that you have. Especially the ones with the neck piece connected to them! That shit is live and in effect!"

Kimberly and Brittany stared at one another for several moments, before Kim shook her head. "No more BET for you, Mia."

Mia pointed toward Kim. "Stop playing."

Brittany walked to the table and flipped through Kimberly's new sketches. "Girl, Mia is right, you need your own shit."

"Get out of here!" Kimberly said, waving her hand and dismissing them.

"I'm serious, Kim!" Brittany told her.

"Me too!" Mia nodded. "Your designs are better than anything in the stores right now. I haven't seen anything in Elle, Ms., Vogue, Essence, Town and Country, Harper's, or Mocha that can touch your stuff. You should really do it, Kimmie."

"It's not like you have anything else to do right now," Brittany reminded her. "You're not getting up and going to work anymore."

"I wouldn't know the first thing about getting started," Kim told them.

"You said that it's your time, right?" Mia asked.

Kim nodded.

"Well, you have to make it your time, you just can't speak that shit into existence," Mia told her. "Get off your ass and get on the internet."

"Go down to city hall and get some information on starting a business," Brittany told her.

"Yeah, I know that the city has business incubators that'll help you along," Mia added.

"And do what? Design, and then what?"

"Have your designs turned into reality," Brittany told her.

"You send them off to Canada or Mexico or The Philippines and have someone make them and ship the finished product back to you." Mia told her.

"Send my designs to a sweatshop in the Philippines, and have someone bootleg my designs?" Kim asked, lifting any eyebrow.

"Girl, you copyright your work, and if you're not comfortable with Mexico or Thailand, or Taiwan, or The Philippines, you do Canada," Brittany told her.

"Oh, I know!" Mia said, bouncing up and down excitedly. "You do Africa! You can find a garment manufacturing firm in Senegal, or the Ivory Coast, or even Liberia, because they could use the money to help them rebuild after the civil wars they've just had. The United States has zero tariffs on textiles and garments imported from Africa in order to help their economies. You can get a great price on the work, and have it shipped over here at a reasonable price, and you won't have to pay any tariffs on the goods!"

"Why do you always have to get political?" Kim asked. "Besides, I'm not sure if I want to support some African sweatshop, any more than I want to support a Philippino one."

"Okay, well then have then sewn in Italy, big money!" Mia said sarcastically.

"Which brings me to the next line on the agenda!" Kim said. "I don't have the money to pay anyone to manufacture my designs. And even if I did, I would have to spend a great deal of time trying to get buyers interested in my products. That would take up all of my time, time which I don't have. Time that I need to run the business and design other ensembles."

"Screw that!" Brittany told her. "Don't do it that way. Take your designs straight to the streets."

"The streets?" Kim recoiled.

"The mean streets of Manhattan, baby!" Brittany said, hi-fiving Mia.

"You can open up your own boutique to sell your own products!" Brittany told her.

"I know a perfect little store front, right in the

fashion district!" Mia said, clasping her hands together. "It's so quaint."

"And how much is this quaint place in the middle of the fashion district going to cost?" Kim asked. She held up her hands. "Wait a minute. It doesn't even matter. I can't afford a place in the middle of the worst neighborhood in Jersey, so it doesn't matter. We're just dreaming."

"Why, Kim?" Mia asked. "Why are we just dreaming?"

"Reality starts off as a dream!" Brittany said excitedly.

"I don't have the money!" Kim told them.

"We can get the money!" Mia told her.

"How?" Kim asked. "I'm not going to my parents! Not for that. There is no way I could ask my mother for that money. She would have a field day gloating."

"I'm not saying go to your mother," Mia told her. "I'm saying, go to your sisters!"

"My sister?" Kim asked.

"No, your *sisters*!" Brittany said, understanding what Mia was getting at.

"I have some money saved up," Mia told her.

"Oh, no!" Kim said, waving her hand and dismissing Mia's offer. "Money and friendship, and business and sisterhood do not mix!"

"We wouldn't be giving you the money," Brittany told her.

Kim shook her head. "I couldn't let you loan me that type of money. God only knows why, or how, or if I would ever be able to pay you back!"

"We wouldn't be loaning it to you either." Mia told her.

"What are you talking about then?" Kimberly asked.

"We would be investors," Brittany explained.

"Yeah," Mia said nodding. "We would be partners in the boutique and the clothing line."

"Partners?" Kim asked skeptically.

Brittany nodded. "The three of us would be equal partners. We would put up the money, and help out on the weekends and after work. You put up the talent, and run things during the day."

Kim shook her head. "Thanks, guys, but I don't know about this. I'm honored that you believe in me enough to do this, but…"

"But my ass, Kimberly!" Mia told her. "You got the talent, and we've got the bread. Why not make it happen. What have we got to lose?"

"How about your money?" Kim told her.

Mia shrugged. "I can always make more."

"And I can always run to Daddy for more," Brittany said with a smile.

"You two really want to put your money into this?" Kim asked.

"I'm writing a check to the company for a hundred grand," Mia told her. "We can go and open up a company bank account tomorrow."

"I'll deposit the same," Brittany told her. "If we need more, I'll deposit more."

"Two hundred grand should get us the building, the display racks, and enough to hire some help," Mia said. "It'll also get us enough garments made to start off really well."

"We'll need some cute purses and shoes!" Brittany told her.

"Right, we can't have a clothing line without some cute bags and shoes!" Mia concurred.

"And we'll need a name!" Brittany said.

"Something catchy!" Mia told them.

They both turned toward Kimberly.

"Our names?" Kim asked. "Our first initials?"

"In alphabetical order?" Mia asked.

"BKM?" Brittany asked.

"BKM Manhattan!" Kimberly suggested.

"BKM Manhattan Couture!" Brittany said.

"I like that!" Mia said, pointing toward Brittany.

"That's it!" Kim said, now growing more animated. "BKM Manhattan Couture!"

"Donna Karan, eat your heart out!" Mia shouted.

"Wait until you see the new leather bag that I'm designing for the company!" Kim told them. She waved her hand through the air in grandiose fashion. "The new BKM Manhattan Couture, Fifth Avenue Bag!"

Mia bounced up and down excitedly. Kimberly and Brittany quickly joined her, and the three of them began to bounce all over the furnishings throughout the room.

"Paris, here we come!" Mia shouted.

"Look out Louis Vuitton!" Brittany shouted.

Kimberly raced to the table and flipped open her design portfolio. "I have all kinds of ideas running through my head!"

Brittany and Mia joined her at the table, peering over her shoulder.

"We can name our bags after the different Avenues," Kim told them. "Their can be a First Avenue Bag, a Second Avenue Bag, and so on and so forth. We can do a Carnegie line of upscale gowns and tuxedos. We can do a Fifth Avenue After Dark collection of tasteful but sexy undergarments for women. We can do a Fifth Avenue Black label of luxury garments, a Fifth Avenue Purple label, a Fifth Avenue Brown Label, all kinds of possibilities! We are going to rock the fashion world!"

"Whoah!" Mia shouted. "That's the Kimmie I know from Princeton!"

Kimberly lifted her pencil and began sketching. She knew that months ago, she wouldn't have even contemplated such a bold move, no matter how convincing Mia and
Brittany were. She was only doing this for one reason, and one reason only. It was because a certain man had told her that she could. He told her that she was worthy, and that she could do anything that she put her mind to. A certain man had built her up, and given her the confidence to do bold things. Quitting her job had been the first step along this path that she knew that she would eventually take. She had just been trying to figure out a way to get a loan, and then ask her Dad for the rest of the money. But now Mia and Brittany had come through for her.

Kimberly peered over her shoulder to see where her friends were. They had resumed painting and decorating their nails. She was free to express herself however she wanted to. She peered up toward the ceiling and closed her eyes.

"Thank you, Sterling," she whispered. Thank you for believing in me, and for giving me the confidence to believe in myself, she thought. Now, if only her other wish would come true. She needed God to give her the chance to see him again, the opportunity to make things right. She was going to have her business, now all she wanted was to get her man back.

Chapter Twenty Nine

BKM Manhattan Couture was a huge success. The store front in Manhattan's fashion district had put them right in the thick of things, and their revenue showed it. They had projected gross revenues of over one million dollars for the fiscal year. Kimberly's designs were all the rage, and she was quickly becoming the talk of the town. She even got the chance to supply Rick Ross, Drake, Jay Z, Lil Wayne, and Jeezy's outfits to various award shows. Kimberly was the hot new designer, BKM Manhattan Couture was the hot new design house, and the boutique stayed busy.

Despite the face that the boutique maintained a healthy crowd, Kimberly noticed her as soon as she walked in. Whereas the boutique's primary customers were older, wealthy, white socialites, she was different. Most of her customers came into the store looking as if they had just stepped out of a

Mary Kay meets Mikimoto Pearls convention, she had a style that was *way* different. Her look was off the charts.

That she was Italian was without question. Her skin was olive in complexion, while her ensemble was something that no one had ever seen before. She recognized the look, though. It had to either be Versace, or Vespasian.

Her olive colored calve length skirt, matched the fitted olive colored suit jacket, as well as her oversized olive colored hat that she wore tilted to the side, and her olive colored high heels. She even wore titanium framed rimless sunglasses, with olive colored lenses. Her entire outfit was fierce, and she knew it, because she walked like it. It wasn't the walk of a fashion model, nor the walk of a high powered executive. It was the walk of a woman who owned the world, and who was used to being pampered by it. And then Kimberly noticed the purse.

It was a Vespasian Mummy Bag, but strangely enough, it wasn't in the usual camel or dark saddle color. This one was olive, and it matched her outfit to a tee. This fact only brought further suspicion to the woman. Who was this superwoman who could order Vespasian's latest bag, in a special color to match her outfit? Something like that would entail sending swatches of the material to the Vespasian design firm, who would have to send the sample to the tannery in England, who would have to match the color exactly, create a special dye, and then dye the leather and send it off to the manufacturer to be sewn into the purse. A regular Mummy Bag was over six thousand dollars. A custom created Mummy Bag had to be at least twice that much. A twelve thousand dollar purse, and an outfit that was about the same price, once the three thousand dollar leather heels were calculated. Who was she?

The diamonds in her ears sparkled like the Christmas Tree at Macy's. She wore a five tiered matching diamond tennis bracelet, a diamond covered Piaget, and a diamond ring on her finger that had to have cost at least a couple of million dollars. And her nails couldn't have been done in the United States.

Kimberly watched as the woman browsed, and then chose her Jungle Bag from BKM's Fifth Avenue Black Collection. It was a black crocodile and boa skin purse, with gold nomenclature, and a black silk lining in the interior. The bag was one of her most popular items. It had been released a week ago, and had sold out three times. Neiman Marcus and Saks Fifth Avenue representatives had come begging for some of the bags. She sold them to the stores at regular price.

Without asking for a price, the woman strolled to the counter, placed the bag on top of it, and pulled out a black American Express Card that matched the purse.

"Excuse me, your bag," Kim said, clearing her throat. "Is that a Vespasian Mummy Bag?"

"Yes it is," the woman said, in a thick Italian accent.

"I've never seen one in that color before," Kimberly told her.

"You won't," she said. "I however, have them in about twenty different colors."

Kim swallowed hard to clear the lump in her throat. "Wow. You must be very fortunate."

"Not really," the woman shrugged. "I designed them."

"I thought that you looked familiar!" Kimberly told her.

"Yes, Kimberly, we met in Las Vegas last year," Gianna told her.

"Wow, you look fantastic!" Kimberly said, examining her. "What are you doing now?"

"Your job," Gianna told her.

"Excuse me?"

Gianna waved her hand around the store. "You should be running the women's line at Vespasian. It is a job that is perfect for you."

Kimberly shook her head. "No, I have my work cut out for me here."

"Vespasian Women would buy BKM Manhattan of course, and roll it into our women's line, and you would run Vespasian Women," Gianna told her. "You could keep an eye on BKM Manhattan, while running the whole show. Vespasian would pay you handsomely for your company of course."

Kim was stunned.

"Your designs need to be seen by the world," Gianna told her. "You're doing well here in your tiny boutique in New York, but all of America, and all of the world should be able to enjoy your work. Vespasian would take your clothes world wide."

"Wow, that's very flattering, but…"

"But nothing. You are very talented. With Vespasian's efficiency, marketing power, connections, and money, you would quickly become a household name." Gianna lifted the Jungle Bag. "This is very nice, very creative, very well put together. The world would love this bag. They would go crazy over this bag in Paris and Milan."

"I can't," Kimberly told her, shaking her head.

"Well, I've talked to you about running the women's line at Vespasian, I've purchased my Jungle Bag, and now for my last piece of business. I love Sterling. He is like an older brother to me. He loves you, and you need to go to him and make things right between the two of you."

"Wait a minute," Kim said, holding up her palm. "Did Sterling send you here?"

"Of course not!" Gianna said offended. "Sterling is not that type of man. It is about time you realized that Sterling is good man."

"Of course you think so, he's your boss. And judging by that jewelry, he's paying you pretty damn good to run Vespasian Woman."

Gianna burst into laughter. "You think this come from company's petty salary? I am Gianna DeMontolo Ferrari Guigaro. I work for Sterling, because I *want* to work, because I love designing. Designing is in my blood. My grandfathers designed beautiful Italian cars. Both the Guigaros and the Ferraris blood runs through my veins. And both the Guigaros and the Ferraris money fills my bank account. No, I am here because I love Sterling, and because he is a great man, who gave a little girl a chance to follow her heart. That is the thing about Sterling. He is a man who gives chances, and who believes in people. Are you worthy of such a man?"

"Of course I am!" Kimberly said indignantly. "It is very presumptive of you to come here and lecture me…"

Gianna waved her hand dismissing Kimberly's statement. "Go to him."

"What?"

"He has flown to Milan, Italy for the young designers conference and fashion show. It is the place where new and unheard of designers go to have their work seen, and to be discovered. It is the place where Sterling discovered me, and gave me my chance. Take your designs with you, and enter them into the show. But most of all, go and find Sterling. Go and find true love."

"What?" Kimberly asked. Things were moving too fast for her.

"You already have the designing eye of an Italian, now I will help you to have the heart and the passion of an Italian woman." Gianna told her. "But to do that, you must give your heart to love."

"I can't just pick up and fly to Italy!" Kimberly told her.

"You can do anything you put your mind to,"

Gianna said with a smile.

Kimberly smiled. She knew that it was Sterling's favorite saying. "What if he doesn't want to see me?"

"Trust me, he wants to see you," Gianna said flatly.

"How do you know? Did he say something?"

"No."

"Well then, how do you know?"

"Because I know Sterling. I know this man's heart."

Kimberly shook her head. "I don't know. What if he's already met someone else?"

"Your insecurity boars me," Gianna told her. "It was cute in the beginning, but now it is tiresome, my dear."

Kimberly recoiled.

Gianna tossed an envelope onto the counter. "Your ticket to Italy, and your pass to get into the show."

"Gianna, I can't!"

"You can and you will," Gianna said turning, and heading for the exit.

"Your receipt!" Kim shouted.

Gianna waved her off. "Keep it, I don't return things. I don't like anymore, I throw away!"

Chapter Thirty

The Bvlgari Hotel Milano was named after the famous Italian designer, and bore his unique touch throughout. The famed hotel was a precious jewel on the Italian landscape; as precious as any created by Bvlgari himself. The hotel's original building dated back to the 18th century, while the private gardens that surrounded the hotel, sat next to a lush botanical garden that dated back to 1774. It was a rarity to find such a lush tropical retreat in the center of any major metropolitan area, and this was part of what made the Bvlgari Hotel Milano magical.

The Hotel sat within Milan's most stylish area. It bordered Via della Spiga on one side, and Via Montenapoleone on another. This gave its patrons access to Milan's finest restaurants and entertainment venues, although it was not as if they would be rushing to leave the comforts of the hotel.

Black Zimbabwe marble ran through the

hotel's common areas, while Vicenza stone and Turkish Aphyon could be found throughout the spa. Solid teak and durmast filled the bedrooms. In each of the suites, special meditation corners complete with Tatami floors were nestled in the corners. The suites also boasted walk-in closets, plasma TV systems, wireless conference telephone systems, high speed internet, and complimentary wireless laptops. And the hotel's main spa was equipped with a gold mosaic swimming pool. The Bvlgari was for the movers and shakers of the world.

The hotel's services were only to be dreamed about. The hotel offered everything from in-room check-in, to complementary luggage packing and unpacking, to in-room dining services, and twenty four hour valet and concierge services. Personal trainers were available, as were personal shoppers in case the well to do patrons were too busy to shop on their own. The hotel even offered image consulting services for their patrons hair and makeup. Luxury car rentals were only a phone call away, as were private planes, helicopters, yachts, and limousines to explore the city's finest escapes. The hotel even offered private tours of gourmet food and wine producers in Northern Italy. Of course all of these services and amenities came at a steep price. A very steep price.

Of course price was no object to Sterling. He stayed in the Bvlgari Suite on the hotel's top floor. It was a suite that offered a view over the historic part of Milan, and of the hotel's gardens. It was a suite that had Brera stone fireplaces, and bathtubs carved from a single block of Bihara Stone that had been imported from Turkey. It was a suite that had been decorated and furnished by none other than Bvlgari himself.

The botanical gardens were where Sterling found refuge away from the hustle and bustle and lights and glamor and glitz of the fashion show. Here, there were no paparazzi. Here, there was only peace and quiet and tranquility. This evening, he shared the gardens with only a few red robins and humming birds. Even the traffic from the surrounding city seemed miles away, as the chirps and whistles and fluttering wings dominated the evening air.

Today's events had been particularly trying. All the paparazzi wanted to know about was his personal life, and when was the Mummy Bag going to be available in other colors besides brown and black. They had been particularly vicious about Kimberly, and whether her new Jungle Bag was the new 'it' bag. They wanted to know how he felt about her launching her clothing line, and how he felt about the The Jungle Bag competing with his Mummy Bag. They had been relentless, shameless even. All he wanted to do now was relax.

"Some hotel," the voice said from behind.

Sterling turned. It was her.

"Kim!" he said shocked. "What are you doing here?"

"I'm in the show," she told him.

"Wow, that's fantastic," Sterling said, stumbling through his words. "Congratulations. I mean on everything. On being in the show, and on your new company."

"Thank you, Sterling," she said with a smile.

"I always knew you could do it."

Kimberly nodded. "I know. And that's the only reason that I could."

"Huh?" Sterling asked. He didn't understand.

"The only reason that I could do even a fraction of the things that I've done, is because of you. You believed in me, Sterling. You gave me the confidence to step out and grab life by the horns."

Sterling shook his head. "You give me too much credit. It was always inside of you."

"It took a good man to bring it out."

Sterling shifted his gaze toward the ground. He didn't know what to say, or how to reply. He didn't know how much of his feelings he should reveal at that point. Was she still upset, was she open to his apology? He didn't know where to take the conversation.

"Thank you, Sterling," Kim said softly. She too, was nervous and unsure of herself, and she was also unsure of his feelings toward her.

"Kim, I just want to say I'm sorry for hurting you, and for causing you any pain," Sterling told her. "I abused your trust, and for that I will be eternally sorry."

Kim shook her head. "No, Sterling, no apologies are necessary. Not from you, anyway. I over reacted. I allowed my past to cloud my judgment, and to influence my future. You are not John, and your past relationships aren't *his* past relationships."

"I should have told you about Third."

"Is that his name?" Kim asked with a smile. "Third?"

"Sterling Williams the Third," Sterling said, returning her smile. He pulled out his wallet and produced a picture of his son.

"Handsome," Kimberly declared. "Looks a

lot like his father."

"Thank you."

"I would love to meet your son, Sterling," Kimberly said nervously.

"You would?" It had taken him by surprise.

Kimberly nodded. "I would. I want to meet him. He's special to you, and that makes him special to me."

Sterling lifted his hand to his face and rubbed his eyes. Things were moving fast. What did all of this mean? Did she want to give their relationship another chance?

"I don't understand, Kim." Sterling told her. "What are you saying?"

"I'm saying that I'm sorry, Sterling."

"You have nothing to be sorry about."

"I'm sorry for hurting you. I'm sorry for bringing *my* past into *our* future. I'm sorry for not recognizing you for the man you really are."

"You don't know what it means to hear you say that."

"But I do have to know, Sterling. I know that this is a messed up question to ask, but I have to ask it."

"Ask me anything."

"Is there anything else, Sterling?" Kimberly

asked, staring into his eyes. "Any more secrets. Anything that I should know about? Anything that could come back and hurt me?"

Sterling shook his head. "There are no more secrets, Kim. Nothing else. At least not on my end."

Kim shook her head. "I have none."

"Are you free?" Sterling asked. "I mean, truly free. Free to love me with everything that you have, with everything that you are? Or is there a part of you that is always going to worry about John, or your history with John, or what John is doing now? I can't be John."

"I wouldn't have it any other way," Kim told him. "I need Sterling. John is a hurter, but my Sterling is a healer. I need my Sterling. The man who builds people up. The man who sees the best in people. The man who gives chances. I'm hoping that he also gives second chances."

"Are you kidding me?" Sterling asked. "I beg you to come back to me."

"You don't have to beg," Kim told him. She dropped to one knee. "I'm the one who is going to plead."

Sterling tried to pull her up, but she resisted. Kimberly produced a ring and held it up. "I have my business, my clothing line, my friends, my family, my health, and a good life, and it's all because of you. What you gave me, words cannot begin to describe. How you make me feel, I can't even begin to explain. You make me feel worthy. You validate my existence. I love you, Sterling. I love being around you, I love waking up in your arms, I love hearing the sound of your voice. I look around these gardens, and I think back to that day on the plantation when you talked about Black love, and how that man took that woman into his arms and healed her. He told her that it was okay, and that they would get through this world together. They built a family out of that love, and despite the monsters of this world, they endured. You are that type of healer, Sterling. God gave that to you. You have that in your soul!"

Tears fell from both of their eyes.

"I want to build that family with you, Sterling. I want to build a love that will endure a lifetime, a love that transcends time and space, a love that is forever."

Sterling nodded.

"I want you to marry me," Kim said through her tears.

Sterling nodded, and wiped the tears from his

eyes. She placed the ring on his finger, and then he took her hand into his and gently pulled her up. Their eyes closed, as the two of them drifted closer. Soon, their lips met, and they kissed one another with a passion that transcended time. They kissed one another with a passion that said their love was ordained by none other than The Man Upstairs. They kissed one another with a passion that said… forever.

Please follow me on Twitter at Twitter.com/CalebAlexander.

Also, like my Facebook author page at Caleb'Thehitfactory'Alexander.

Check out these other great titles by Caleb Alexander.

Boyfriend # 2
Eastside
Belly of the Beast
Deadly Reigns IV
Deadly Reigns V
Baby Baller
Two Thin Dimes

www.ingramcontent.com/pod-product-compliance
Lightning Source LLC
Chambersburg PA
CBHW071050250626
47159CB00002B/429